Truth or Dare?

Truth or Dare?

Dwayne S. Joseph

www.urbanbooks.net

Urban Books, LLC
78 East Industry Court
Deer Park, NY 11729

Truth or Dare? Copyright © 2011 Dwayne S. Joseph

ISBN 13: 978-1-60162-330-0
ISBN 10: 1-60162-330-5

First Trade Paperback Printing October 2011
Printed in the United States of America

10 9 8 7 6 5 4 3 2 1

Distributed by Kensington Publishing Corp.
Submit Wholesale Orders to:
Kensington Publishing Corp.
C/O Penguin Group (USA) Inc.
Attention: Order Processing
405 Murray Hill Parkway
East Rutherford, NJ 07073-2316
Phone: 1-800-526-0275
Fax: 1-800-227-9604

Acknowledgments

Thanks to God . . . a new adventure is about to begin. I'm waiting to see what you have in store. To my wife and kids . . . this one took me away for a lot of hours. I appreciate the patience. To my family and friends . . . thanks for having my back and being the best. To my special crew of readers: Nancy Silvas, Portia Cannon, Cheryl Francis . . . thank you for taking the time and the great feedback. To the readers and book clubs (Mom, I truly appreciate you and the Circle Of Women) . . . thank you all for the love and support you continue to show me. I'm honored that you all take the time to hit me up on Facebook and in e-mail to let me know that you enjoy the storylines and the dark twists and turns! Knowing that you do, keeps me pushing the envelope. To Victoria Christopher Murray, Eric Pete, La Jill Hunt, Anna J. . . . thank you guys for the friendship and support. Let's keep it going! To Brian Smith, Moses Miller, Marc Lacey, Vincent Alexandria, Ricky Teems & Jihad . . . I cannot tell you enough how honored I am to be a part of the Love Literature Tour!

To my G-Men! My son's got his helmet. I'm preparing him to wear the Big Blue someday! Let's get it!

Hit me up and remember: If you don't know . . . you will!

Dwayne S. Joseph
Djoseph21044@yahoo.com
www.facebook.com/Dwayne-S-joseph

Truth or Dare?

Jess sighed as she turned on her laptop. In a few minutes, she was going to tell Jayson that two weeks wasn't going to happen, because it couldn't. Not again. A one-night stand: technically, that's all their night was. She felt bad about that, not because it was the right thing to do, but rather because Jayson was a good man who didn't deserve to have that done to him. So, two days ago, she had backed out and skipped her seminar to avoid him. But now, she sat ready and determined to take the first step toward redemption because she needed to be able to look her husband in the eye again. She needed to be able to look at her girls and feel the pride she felt before she'd done the unthinkable. Until she closed the book to a very dark chapter in her life, however short it had been, she couldn't face Esias; she couldn't be her daughters' example. So, as Windows loaded, Jess sat still, ready and desperate to get it over with.

She'd lost herself over the course of seven weeks and, as she had, her marriage had suffered. Esias was an imperfect man who was absolutely perfect for her, and for the past few weeks, she had treated him like shit. He didn't deserve that. Her girls hadn't deserved to see the man who loved them more than anything in the world get half-assed treatment.

Jess took a breath, and then moved her arrow to the AOL icon. Jayson would be waiting for her; she knew. She didn't know how he was going to take what she had to say; that after tonight, the game was officially over. But, she couldn't worry about that. The time had come to get back on the right path.

Truth or Dare?

Chapter 1

Jess was stressed. She'd missed the deadline to withdraw from her classes for the semester, and now she
was a week behind in both of her programming classes.
She groaned and ran her hands through her short,
Halle Berry-styled hair. She needed a haircut, but that
was the last item on her laundry list of things she had
to take care of.

She looked at the seventeen-and-a-half-inch screen
on her MacBook and groaned again as she listened to
her online professor speak, while her classmates furiously typed comments and questions that prompted
the professor to babble off more technical jargon that
she didn't understand.

She ran both hands through her hair and scratched
her scalp, not because it was itching, but, rather, just
because it was as close to driving a knife through her
heart with her own hand as she would get.

Chicken, she thought. *Just go and get the damn
knife. It would be a hell of a lot easier to just end it that
way, than to sit through a frustrating semester with
high blood pressure while you die slowly. Chicken!*

Jess took a breath and released it heavily. She wasn't
ready for this. Mentally, she was already at the beach,
Six Flags, the park, or just on her couch with her legs
stretched out and her Victoria Christopher Murray
novel in her hands. Stress still existed, but it was just
the typical work-related stress; the bills-that-needed-

to-be-paid stress; and the two, overly dramatic and all-too-whiney-little-girls stress. She could deal with those stressors with no problem. What she couldn't deal with was another eight weeks of mundane seminars, mandatory participation sessions, quizzes, weekly assignments due at the stroke of midnight, and most important, the sleepless nights.

Mentally, she wasn't prepared for that, which is why she'd tried to take the summer off to recharge her battery that had long been drained. But, she'd read the e-mail from her academic advisor giving her instructions and withdrawal deadlines incorrectly and now she was two assignments, four seminars, and six class participations behind.

Jess let out another wounded moan as she scratched her scalp again, and then pulled down on the back of her neck. She was exhausted. Work was as stressful as ever, the kids were becoming increasingly more demanding, and her husband was becoming more unavailable, leaving her virtually no chance to relax in the evening before she sat down in front of her laptop. She took a glance at the time in the bottom right corner of her screen. It was a quarter to eleven. Fifteen minutes to go before she'd begin to tackle attempting to get herself caught up. Fifteen minutes before she'd begin the ritual of going to bed well after one in the morning, only to get up at five to get ready for work.

She wanted to cry.

And perhaps she would have, had an AOL instant message window not suddenly appeared on her screen.

R u as lost as I am??

Jess looked at the message with the strange font, bunched her eyebrows together, and then looked at the screen name of the person who'd sent it. Jayson Winston. The only reason she had downloaded the instant messenger was because it had been a requirement for her classes. If and when it was used, which was rare, it was only during class. She looked at the name again. Jayson Winston. She recognized it from her PHP (Hypertext Preprocessor) class. She thought about closing the IM window. After all, she and Jayson had never exchanged words before, but the question had been a comforting one because, for the first time, she'd felt as though she weren't alone. She nodded her head, let out an "Uh-huh," and then typed a reply.

I'm beyond lost! Ahhh!

She hit send with a smile.

Seconds later, Jayson replied.

The prof lost me after the first 5 minutes!

Jess chuckled.

At least u made it 4 5! I've been lost since I signed on. I missed the last 2 seminars!

Damn! Why?

I thght I had withdrawn in time, then found out I hadn't. Now I can't or else I'll hve to pay 4 the classes!

That sucks!

Tell me abt it. I have no clue what the professor is tlking abt, and the textbooks don't help worth a damn. I feel like the village idiot compared 2 everyone else.

LOL! Well, at least now u knw u hve a neighbor in the village!

LOL! Sorry u r struggling 2, but it is nice 2 knw I'm not alone.

I'm Jayson Winston by the way.

Jess smiled.

I'm Jessica Richards. But I go by Jess.

I like tht. Sounds cool, stylish. Nice 2 meet u, Jess.

Nice 2 meet u 2, Jayson.

There was a pause of messages for a few minutes, and when creaking and closing doors began to sound—

indications that students were logging out of AOL—
Jess wondered if Jayson too had called it a night. She
looked at her friend list and saw that he was still logged
in. She didn't know why, but she smiled.

A few more creaking and slamming door sounds
went off as the professor told everyone good night. Jess
sighed. "Nice talking to you, Jayson," she said with soft
disappointment.

She scrolled her arrow to the AOL menu and clicked
on the drop down, giving the option to click to sign off.

Hey, Jess . . . u still thre?

Jess's index finger had been inches away from going
down on her sensory pad to log out of the messenger.
The corners of her mouth curled upward.

I am. Was jst abt 2 log out. Thght u had gone.

No . . . sorry. Brkng news came on ESPN abt my NY
Giants.

I take it ur a big fan?

Sheeit! I bleed blue!

LOL.

U in2 sports?

Yup! Die-hard Stlrs fan here.

Stlrs schmlrs. It's all abt the Big Blue!

LOL! All I hve 2 say 2 tht is 6 rings!

Yeh, yeh.

Stlrs, baby! Woot woot!

LOL! So were u born and raised in P'burgh?

I'm actually a New Yorker. Born and raised in the
Bronx.

Oh yeh? And yet u like the Stlrs?

My husband is frm Pittsburgh. He got me in2 the
game.

Hubby's lucky. Not many guys hve wives tht get in2
the game, especially if thy wrn't in2 it bfre.

Jess frowned as she thought about her husband, Esias. Hectic schedules, her online classes, and his side career as a budding producer had them at a disconnect for the past year and a half. She didn't reply.

After a few seconds, Jayson sent another message.

So ... a hubby ... any kids?

Jess smiled.

2 grls.

Lil princesses. Wht's their names?

Jeanette and Jasmine.

Prtty.

Wht abt u? Married? Kids?

Hell, no! I'm proud 2 say I'm in the minority.

Minority?

I'm a brotha with no girlfriend and no kids!

Wow! What's wrong with u? Gay?

Hell, no!

Lol!

Lol. I hve some things I want 2 accomplish. I'm not tryn 2 hve kids til I do. Besides .... I hvn't found the rght woman yet.

Sigh. The world could use more black men with tht mentality. Especially the younger ones.

Yeah.

The sounds of keys rattling announced themselves.

Jess looked up. Esias was home. She shouldn't have, but she sighed, and then typed quickly.

Hey ... hve 2 run. We'll tlk again.

Awww ... OK.

Hve a good night.

Jess closed the messenger window before Jayson could reply, and then signed out of AOL just as Esias walked into their home. Her heart was beating heavily, and beads of perspiration had formed on her forehead. *Why?* she wondered. It wasn't as though she were doing anything wrong, just casual conversation. Yet, despite the rationale, the guilty feeling remained. She logged out of the classroom, and then closed her laptop down. As she did, Esias walked into the living room.

"Hey," he said, his voice weary.

"Hey," Jess replied.

Esias put a stack of blank CDs he'd been holding in his hand down on the dining table, and then walked over to her. He was still dressed in his business attire: black slacks, white dress shirt, baby blue tie undone. She always liked when he dressed up. He leaned down and gave her a kiss on her lips. "I didn't mean to take so long, but I was in a zone. Sorry."

Jess shrugged. "This was one of those rare nights I was able to get Jeanette and Jas in bed before my seminar."

Esias gave a nod of approval, and then stood erect and stretched. "Are they asleep?"

"Yeah. But, you need to wake them up to go to the potty."

"OK," Esias said.

Jess pushed her chair back and stood up. "So, you got a lot done?"

Esias nodded. "Yeah. Got three tracks done, one hip-hop, one more of a Linkin Park kind of a track, and then a throwback baby maker one. Anxious for you to hear them."

"Can't wait."

"How was your seminar?"

Jess groaned. "Frustrating. I'm so completely lost."

Esias raised his eyebrows up and down. "You'll catch up."

Jess sighed. "I don't know. With the other classes, I at least felt like I could when I got lost. This is the first time I feel like I might fail."

Esias walked into the kitchen and opened the refrigerator. "You won't," he said.

"I can't," Jess said. "We can't afford to pay the school any money right now. Speaking, of which, our turn-off notice for BG&E has to be paid by this Friday."

Esias nodded. "We'll take care of it when I get paid on Thursday. How much is it again?"

"Four hundred twenty dollars."

Esias snapped his head up in her direction. "What? How the hell is it so much? I thought you paid last month's bill."

"I didn't do the whole thing. I only paid what we owed from the previous month."

"So we'll pay what we owe from last month again."

"I tried when we got the notice. But we've been behind for too long. They want the whole thing now."

Esias slammed the refrigerator shut. "Goddamn," he said. "Do you get paid this week?"

"No."

"Shit. That's most of my fucking check."

Jess sighed. "Yup."

"Goddamn," Esias whispered again. He dragged his hand down over his face and pulled down on his chin. "Goddamn." He planted his hands on his hips, dropped his chin to his chest, and stood still for a few seconds.

Jess frowned. They both made decent money, had relatively little debt, yet they couldn't seem to get ahead.

A minute or two passed, and then Esias turned to her. "I have to get this demo done," he said. "I have some people interested in hearing more of my music. The sooner I can get it in their hands, the sooner I think I can get a deal and get some more money in here."

"That would be nice."

"So does that mean you won't be giving me any grief about needing more time in the studio?"

Jess shook her head. "As long as you're back before my seminars begin, and you know that Mondays and Tuesdays are off-limits, then handle your business."

Esias turned his palms up to the ceiling. "How do you expect me to handle my business when you're giving me restrictions like that?"

"Why do you have to look at it like that, Esias? I'm just asking for some give-and-take."

"Didn't you just say it would be nice if I brought more money in here?"

"Yes, I did."

"So how do you expect me to come home before your seminars? And how could you say I can't have Mondays or Tuesdays?"

Jess curled her lips. *Unbelievable*, she thought. "Esias . . . I need you home before my seminars because nights like tonight don't happen often. And I need you here on Mondays and Tuesdays because those are the nights my assignments are due. It's not about restricting you. It's about you compromising with me."

Esias let out a heavy breath. "Compromise, compromise," he said, tossing his hands up to the ceiling. "I've been compromising ever since you started taking your classes. Honestly, I could have been done with a demo by now if I didn't have to compromise so damn much."

Jess closed her eyes a fraction. "Esias, all I'm asking for is some consideration. Work is stressful enough as it is. I don't think it's unfair of me to ask you to compromise."

"Work is stressful for me too, Jess, but I need time to handle my business."

"Esias . . . I am behind in both of my classes, and I'm struggling to catch up. I know you need your time, but

I need your time too. The kids don't act the same when you're not around; you know that. So yes, on Mondays and Tuesdays I need you here to help me get them together so I can complete my assignments."

"I need to get this demo done, Jess."

"And I need to pass my classes!"

Jess stared at her husband, while he stared back at her with a set jaw. This was a constant battle between them. One that neither side ever really won. One that was helping to widen the disconnect. Jess took a deep breath and let it out slowly, and as she did, she found herself wishing that she could rewind the clock to twenty minutes earlier when she had been chatting with Jayson Winston.

Jayson Winston. A stranger she'd never met. She shouldn't have been thinking about him; shouldn't have been wondering where he lived, what he was doing, or what he looked like. She shouldn't have been at all, but she was.

She took another breath, let it out as a sigh, and said, "I'm not in the mood to argue, Esias. I have too much to do." Without waiting for him to reply, she opened her laptop, flipped open her textbook, which really was useless, and pretended to get back to work.

Jayson Winston.

He shouldn't have been, but he was on her mind.

Chapter 2

Tell me why I took this class again?

Jess chuckled. I'm still tryn 2 figure out why I did.

It was Wednesday night. Seminar night for PHP class. Usually it was a seminar she dreaded. Now it was an hour-long session she thought about and looked forward to.

All because of Jayson.

Their first chat had occurred during class. The second time they spoke had been during seminar as well, but when the professor said, "Good night," and all of the other students logged off, she and Jayson continued to converse. Only when she finally gave in and looked at the clock to see just how little sleep she was going to get before she had to get up for work did she go to bed. Their third conversation started one hour before class, went through it, and lasted for three hours after. Each time they spoke, Jess smiled more, and the more she smiled, the more she wanted to speak.

Technically, there wasn't anything wrong with what she was doing. She was just chatting with a friend; a male friend; and for far longer than she should have been.

But it was just chatting.

At least, that's what she told herself over and over when her conscience mouthed off in her ear about how she was betraying vows she'd made five years ago. Just chatting. Talking. They were two classmates helping to keep each other afloat when they both felt as though they were going to drown.

Jess smiled as Jayson's reply to what she'd said popped into the messenger window.

We met. Maybe tht's why we took it?

She looked at Jayson's words. They'd met. Two people in a class that neither of them wanted to be in. Strangers walking toward each other from opposite ends of the same road.

Destiny. *Could it have been?*

She shook her head. Destiny had led to a happy hour hangout after a long, frustrating week at work, where her coworker introduced her to her good friends who'd just recently moved to the city. Destiny had her and her coworker's tall, slender, and very attractive friend talking to each other easily, as though that hadn't been the first time they'd met. Destiny then took them on several dates, that evolved into a two-year relationship, which then morphed into marriage a year later, that was now going on five years with two demanding little girls.

Destiny. Fate. Meant to be. She'd never experienced a connection like the one she had with Esias. Now she was sitting in front of her laptop, staring at words that had far more truth to them than they should have.

They'd met.

She didn't want them to, but her fingers typed, May-be, anyway.

And then her heart began to beat heavily and, again, she tried to ignore the words of her conscience. Nothing wrong. They were just two friends chatting as there'd never been a time when they didn't speak.

Where's ur hubby?

Wild horses ran beneath Jess's chest as she took a breath and held it. Esias was at the studio again, trying to make his dream happen. He wanted to be the next top producer. The man behind the scenes raking in all of the real money. Wednesdays, Thursdays, and Fridays were his nights to go to the studio right after work during the week. These were the nights Jess didn't have to cram to get assignments posted by midnight. Two of the three nights—Wednesday and Thursday—were the nights she had seminar. The schedule was too convenient, and she knew what her reply needed to be.

He's not here.

Her conscience screamed in her ear.

R ur grls in bed?

Jess thought about how she'd mastered the art of getting them fed, bathed, and in bed a half hour before her seminar began. Sleeping soundly, she typed.

So essentially it's just u and me?

Heart thumping, temperature rising, conscience yelling, Jess replied, Essentially ... yes.

Being alone ... it's an interesting concept.

Jess took a slow breath. Is it? she typed with an exhale.

Very.

Jess raised her eyebrows and breathed out again. *This is crazy,* she thought. You don't even know what he looks like. She typed, Hmm.

Truth or dare?

Jess stared at the question, surprised by the words. *Leave it alone,* her conscience begged. *Don't play this game. Put your focus back on your schoolwork. Be smart and safe. Avoid the puddle-and-the-ripple effect that would spread if you make a choice. You have a good marriage, despite the widening distance, despite the lackluster routine. Don't be foolish!*

Dare.

She hadn't meant to type the word, but somewhere in-between her conscience's warning and a desire that she couldn't seem to quell, the word had appeared as her response.

Wow! I didn't expect tht.

What did u expect?

I don't knw. I guess 4 u 2 b safe and either not answer or just pick truth.

Jess thought about her response for a moment, then typed. I play it safe all the time . . .

So r u saying playing w/ me is dangerous?

Jess smiled. She couldn't remember the last time she had flirted with someone. Hmm . . . I get the feeling it could b, she responded.

Lol! U hvn't gotten the feeling yet.

Jess felt a tingle between her legs, which she knew was just ridiculous, since she'd never even seen Jayson before. *Just words*, she thought. *Calm down.*

She cleared her throat and typed.

So wht's the dare? And should I b scared?

Lol! Defntly nothing 2 b afrd of.

We'll see. So . . . my dare?

Ur dare.

Yes. My dare.

Does ur cell hve a camera?

Doesn't everyone's?

True. OK . . . so ur dare.

My dare . . . is?

Tke a pic and snd it 2 me.

A pic? Of wht?

Of u.

Me?

Yes.

Hmm. I don't knw . . .

U pckd dare, rmembr?

Jess chuckled. I do.

OK thn.

Hmm . . . wht exctly do u wnt 2 see?

Lol! Tht's a loaded qstn.

Mmm-hmm. I see where ur mind is.

I jst said it was a loaded qstn. U took my words and gve thm a diff meaning. Maybe ur mind is the I tht's somewhere else.

Jess smiled. I don't thnk so.

LOL! So . . . my pic?

Wht did u want 2 see again?

U and these qstns. Lol!

Jess laughed and shook her head. Funny.

Ha-ha . . . OK 4 ur dare . . . I wnt a pic of . . .

Of?

Ur . . .

My?

Face.

My face?

Yes. I wnt 2 put a face wth the name.

Hmm I like my anonymity though.

I'm sure u do. But u chose dare.

Grr . . .

LOL! So r u gng 2 do it?

Jess's conscience screamed *NO!* Told her to close the window, to think about school. She was still behind, though she had caught up considerably. She needed to stop chatting, because it was just wrong on too many levels!

Her conscience yelled, begged, cursed. Jess typed. OK.

So after I tke ths pic . . . wht exctly r u gng 2 do wth it?

I'm gng 2 admire it.

Admire, huh? And wht if I'm ugly? I bet u won't b admiring it thn.

Something tells me I won't hve 2 worry abt tht.
O really? U seem pretty confident abt tht.
Jst a feeling I hve.

Jess thought about his response to her very similar reply. She smiled—a devilish grin—and then typed.

U hvn't felt anything yet.
LOL!

Jess looked around her living room as though the walls were paying close attention so that when they gossiped they would be able to recount every detail of her conversation accurately like someone pressing record on a tape recorder. She shook her head. So wrong. She knew.

So r u gng 2 send it?
Wht if I tell u tht the camera on my phone jst broke?
Hve u ever seen back to the future?
Who hasn't?
Well in that case . . . thn I'd hve 2 call u a chicken!!
LOL!

Jess laughed and reached for her cell phone sitting beside her laptop. She ran her thumb across the screen. A picture. Of her face. "Harmless," she said aloud. A response to her conscience's insistent warning. "It's just my face."

She looked at her MacBook's monitor. Jayson had typed another message.

Jess . . . r u still thre?

Don't reply. It was the right thing to do. She looked at her phone and wiped fingerprint smudges away. "Just my face," she said again. She leaned forward in her chair and used one finger to type. B rght bck.

She rose from her chair, took her phone, and went into the bathroom. She had pictures stored already. Her with the girls. Her with Esias. Some with her girlfriends. If she was going to do something like this, one of those was what she should send. Particularly one with her and her husband.

So knowing that, why was she sprucing up her hair with water? Why was she applying foundation and putting on her lipstick?

Her conscience spoke.

She drowned out the sound by turning on the fan.

Minutes later, she was posing, yet insisting that she wasn't at the same time, and taking a series of five shots. When she was finished, she scrolled through the photographs. She hit delete on the first, not liking the way her slender nose looked. The second picture was gone just as quickly. Drunk wasn't cute. The third picture was OK, though the freckles on her cheeks were a little too noticeable. The fourth photo never had a chance. Her full lips looked like they'd been stung by bees.

The fifth and final shot . . .

She stared at it. Her brown eyes were focused, staring into the camera, a hint of seduction in them. Where had that come from? She didn't know, since she hadn't been going for that. Her lips looked . . . inviting. The strands of her hair were in place. Her forehead didn't shine. The angle of the camera on her good side was just right.

She went back to the third picture, scrutinized it momentarily, and then hit delete before turning off the fan, giving her conscience's voice its volume back, and going back to her laptop.

Bck. R u still thre?

Absolutely!

She smiled.

Did u tke the pic?

I did.

R u sure u wnt 2 see me? U might b disappointed.

I highly doubt it.

OK. Don't say I didn't warn u though.

Lol. OK.

So ... where do I send it?

Jayson typed his number.

Jess's conscience begged her again to turn away from the path she was about to walk down.

Instead, she attached Jayson's number to the picture.

Don't do it! Nothing good is going to come of this.

She took a breath, exhaled, and hit send as goose bumps rose on her skin.

And then there was a noise at the front door. The doorknob being turned.

Jess's heart dropped into the pit of her stomach, and before she even realized she was doing it, she exited out of the messenger and put her phone down. Thirty seconds later, Esias walked into the living room with his guitar hanging over his shoulder, a smile spread wide on his face.

"Hey."

Jess took a short breath and said, "Hey, babe." Her eyes went down to her phone and instantly she regretted what she'd done. *Please don't reply*, she thought.

Esias walked over to her and planted his lips firmly against hers. He kissed her deeply, parting her lips deftly with his tongue. His kisses were always something she loved and responded to without fail, but at that moment, guilt held her back. Esias pulled away and looked at her. "You still have your makeup and lipstick on?"

"I never wiped it off," Jess answered quickly.

Esias nodded with a slightly cocked eyebrow. "OK . . . so how was your seminar?"

"Frustrating."

"Are you getting a grasp of things at all?"

It was wrong, but the word "grasp" brought Jayson to her mind. She shrugged. "Maybe a little."

Esias moved behind her and began to massage her shoulders. "Don't stress too much," he said kneading her tight muscles. "You'll get it just like you always do." He leaned forward and kissed the side of her neck. It was her erogenous zone. He knew it well.

She wanted to respond, but the guilt she was feeling wouldn't allow it.

She stiffened her back and said, "So how was the studio?"

"Great," he replied, working the kinks out. "I have a couple of local rappers who laid down some verses to one of my tracks. They can really flow. As soon as I finish mixing it, I want you to hear it."

Jess tried to breathe as evenly as she could as she looked at her phone, praying again for Jayson to not send her a reply.

Esias worked his thumbs into the muscles of her shoulder blade. Any other night she'd close her eyes, drop her chin to her chest, moan and tell him that if the music didn't work out for him, he had a future in massage therapy. But tonight wasn't like any other night. She shifted in her seat. "Are you hungry?"

Esias let go of her shoulders. "Yeah," he said moving from behind her. "Did you make anything?"

Jess nodded. "It's in the fridge in Tupperware. Rice and chicken."

"Sounds good. I haven't eaten since lunch. Do you mind warming a plate for me while I go to the bathroom?"

Jess shook her head. "No."

Esias leaned forward and gave her another deep, loving kiss. "I love you," he said as he pulled away.

Jess smiled. "I love you too."

Esias gave her another kiss, and then headed to the bathroom. When the door closed, she quickly grabbed her phone and powered it down. Jayson hadn't replied yet, which meant he must have known it wasn't safe to. Jess exhaled a breath of relief and got up to fix her husband's plate. As she did, her conscience repeated over and over again: *I told you so. I told you so.*

Chapter 3

Jayson smiled. He'd hit the jackpot. The mother load. She was *the one*. The ultimate catch. The kids were only a slight negative, but that could be taken care of.

Jess.

Jayson closed his eyes momentarily, leaned his head back against the leather of his chair, and exhaled her name away.

Jess.

Whispering it was like sweet relief.

Jess.

He opened his eyes, raised his cell phone, and stared at the face of an angel. *Beautiful*, he thought. *Stunning*. The gods had truly been smiling down upon him, for they'd delivered the one he'd been searching for all his life.

Jayson smiled again as he stared at Jess's soft doe eyes. She was looking at him with want, with desire. Her eyes gave him the chills. So did her lips. Full, pursed, eager. They wanted his lips on hers; he knew it. He felt it. He felt her.

He forced himself to look away from her inviting photo and looked over to the monitor of his laptop. Jess had logged out of the messenger without a good-bye again. Her husband must have come home. Esias. A pencil pusher/wannabe Dr. Dre.

Jayson twisted his mouth into a sneer. Jess deserved better. A woman of her caliber deserved more. A man that would be there to take care of her every need, her every desire. She should never want for anything. But she did have wants because she was a neglected woman. And that pissed Jayson off. He would never leave Jess alone. Ever. He would sacrifice whatever dreams he had to ensure that Jess would feel safe and secure, because that's the type of man he was. That's the type of man his mother raised him to be. One who gave his all for the woman he loved.

Esias did nothing of the sort.

He left his wife, the woman he supposedly loved, alone after a hard day's work to deal with the house and the kids by herself. And then somehow, after exhausting herself holding things down, she was supposed to have the physical and mental energy required to tackle her schoolwork?

Bullshit. That's what Esias and his supposed love for her was full of. Bullshit.

Jayson ground his teeth together. It was hard waiting, but soon, Jess was going to be his and only his because she was going to come to the realization that she couldn't be without him. Soon. In due time. It was inevitable.

Jayson and Jess sitting in a tree. K-I-S-S-I-N-G. First comes love. Then comes Esias and the kids' nonexistence. Then comes the happily ever after.

He wanted to send Jess a reply. He wanted to tell her how beautiful she was. How she was the figment of every desire he'd ever had. That Halle, Rihanna, Beyoncé, and Alicia had nothing on her. But he couldn't. He didn't want to cause her any unnecessary drama, so he would wait until they talked again, which they most certainly would.

Jayson smiled again, then took a deep breath and exhaled as he stared into Jess's gorgeous face again. *Absolutely and impeccably flawless.* His temperature rose as he looked at her. His blood flowed. It was a good thing he was naked.

As Jess looked at him, her hands stroked his manhood and sent ripples through him—jolts of electric stimulation that culminated in orgasmic waves at his nerve endings.

He closed his eyes as she showed him just how much she yearned for him. How ravenous her hunger for him was. It was an amazing feeling. Otherworldly.

Ding.

Jayson opened his eyes. The ding was notification that an instant message had appeared. Jess had come back.

He looked at the screen, and his smile fell away. It wasn't Jess. It was Debra from his Network Administration class. Another neglected woman yearning to be satisfied. He had numerous photographs of her in his phone. She was no Jess, but until he had the woman of his dreams in his arms, she would do. At least until he was tired of her, which, with Jess's presence, would be very, very soon.

He sat forward and read Debra's message.

Jayson . . . r u thre? My husband's gone. I'm in need.

He clenched his fist. Debra had disturbed Jess from being able to get him to the point of no return. He was in need too. He typed, I'm here and I wnt 2 gve u the real thing.

Mmmm. I wnt tht sooooo bad.

Thn let me gve it 2 u.

I'm ready! Whn?

Tonight.

Tonight???

Yeh. Tonight. I'm in town.

In town???? Whre? Here in Houston?

Yeh. I had a business mtng this mrng.

U should hve told me sooner.

I was busy all day. I nvr had a chance 2.

Ur here!!! I'm in shock.

In 2 much of a shock 2 let me gve it 2 u?

No! But . . . I can't. I don't hve a babysitter.

Hve u ever fckd in the backseat of a car?

Lol. It's been awhile.

I hve an Esclde. Blck wth extrmly tinted windows. R u in a house or an apt?

A house. Why?

U'd b within earshot of ur kids if I came and prkd acrss the street.

Ur insane. I hve neighbors.

Ths is the ultimate dare 4 u, Deb.

Jayson waited as Debra contemplated doing what he knew she was going to do. What they all did.

I can't believe ur here! Whn do u leave?

Tmrrw mrng. 7 am.

U only came 4 I nght?

I nght only.

When r u going 2 come bck?

Not 4 a lng while.

Another few seconds of contemplation.

How dark r ur tints?

It's like looking in2 the nghttme sky w/out the moon, the stars, or the clouds. Drkr than pitch blck.

Hmmm.

R u in need, Deb?

Yessss.

Well, I'm here.

Yes u r.

Send me ur addrss.

OK.

Jayson put her address into his phone as she sent it over.

I can't believe I'm doing this.

I can, Jayson thought. He typed, I'll b thre in 30, and then logged out of the messenger and leaned his head back. Debra wanted the real thing. He did too. He looked at Jess's photo again. In due time. It was destiny.

He got up to get ready for his backseat adventure.

Chapter 4

"So how are your classes going?"

Jess flatlined her lips and moaned.

"That bad, huh?"

She rolled her eyes and released a stressed breath. "Prior to three weeks ago, on a scale of one to ten, with ten being the worst, that bad was a fifty. Now, since I'm caught up with my assignments, it's at about twenty."

"Ouch."

Jess raised her eyebrows. "Yeah, 'ouch' is an understatement. I swear, Melissa, I wish to God I didn't have to worry about paying back for my classes right away by dropping this semester. The stress and frustration are killing me!"

Melissa gave her an apologetic half smile. "I'm sorry," she said sympathetically.

Jess frowned. "So am I." She took a sip of hot coffee she had sitting in front of her, wincing when the hot liquid hit her lips.

Melissa drummed long, pink-colored fingernails on the top of the marble countertop of the island they were seated around. "That really sucks that they wouldn't let you withdraw for the semester without penalty."

Jess sighed and shrugged her shoulders. "It was my fault. If I would have only read the e-mail from my advisor properly . . ."

"Yeah, but still . . . you only missed the deadline by one damn week. You work full-time, you're a wife and a mother. You have a full schedule. They could have bent the rules just a little."

Jess shrugged again. "Maybe, but if they bend them for me, then they'd have to bend them for everyone else."

Melissa sucked her large teeth and waved a bangle-covered hand dismissively through the air. "Oh, please . . . I doubt if anyone else in that class has the kind of schedule you have."

Jess cocked her eyebrows again. "I don't know. They might. There are people from all walks of life in class."

Melissa sucked her teeth again. "Well, I'm sure they don't have the same responsibilities."

Jess raised a shoulder.

"Have you reached out to your instructor for help?"

"I have, but he's not very helpful at all."

"What about your classmates?"

"What about them?" Jess asked, staring at her friend.

"Don't you speak to them?"

Jess looked at her friend. They'd met twelve years ago at Audrey Cohen College in the city. Jess had been a freshman. Melissa, a senior. They had Speech 101 together, a requirement for the communication degree they were both working toward. Though from different backgrounds—Melissa, a white female from the suburbs of Harrisburg, Pennsylvania, and Jess, born and raised in the projects of the Bronx—they had similar personalities and had bonded instantly. Over the course of their friendship, they helped to open each other's mind to different things. Jess credited Melissa with helping her see that there was a world that existed past the projects that consumed its residents, while Melissa owed her mentally tough, no-nonsense attitude to Jess's constant battle against the naivety that used to define her. Twelve years strong, they were best friends and sisters who'd been there for each other through the best and the worst of times.

Melissa was a half-Greek, borderline Amazon female, with a large hooked nose, slanted blue eyes outlined with too much eyeliner, and thick lips that spread wide like Julia Roberts when she smiled. Slightly overweight, she was attractive but had a tendency to conceal her beauty by wearing too much makeup in the constant quest for a flawless appearance.

Jess studied her sister-girl as Melissa waited for Jess to answer. Did she speak to anyone in her class? She had never hesitated to confide in Melissa before. When she needed an ear to divulge information about drama in her life, it was Melissa she went to. When she'd made the decision to drop out of college, Melissa had known long before Jess's parents had. Melissa's ear and ability to keep secrets had always been something Jess counted on, but never before had she had a secret of this caliber: chatting and a fulfilled dare with a classmate she'd never seen or met.

Jess knew that Melissa loved Esias like a long-lost brother, and no matter how she would try to divulge what she'd done, she was positive that Melissa wasn't going to take it well. She shook her head. "Not really."

"Really?"

"Yes. Why do you sound so surprised?"

"I thought you said you use AOL messenger in your class?"

Jess nodded. "We're required to have it, but I don't communicate with anyone outside of posting discussion questions and answers."

"Why not? One of them might really be able to help you."

"I'm not into chatting," Jess answered, thinking of her lengthy exchanges with Jayson.

"Who said anything about chatting? I'm talking about reaching out for help."

Jess resisted again. "I'm just not comfortable with talking to someone I've never met or seen."

"But don't you speak with your instructor who you've never seen?"

"That's different."

Melissa laughed. "Girl, you're crazy. I'm talking about sending someone a message for assistance, not to hook up." She laughed again.

"So . . ." Jess said, studying her closely, "I guess you are into the chat phenomenon?"

"Chat phenomenon?" Melissa said, her eyes opening wide. "The word *online* doesn't exist without the word *chat*."

Jess took a sip of her tea, shrugged again, and said, "You know how I am when it comes to computers."

Melissa sighed. "Yes, I do know. I was shocked when you told me you were going to start taking online classes."

"I wanted to go back and finish school. I just couldn't do it and be away from the kids. Online was just sensible."

"And you're still the only person in the world without a Facebook page!"

"It's enough for me to be online for my classes. I don't have time to be on Facebook. I don't need it anyway."

Melissa rolled her eyes. "Not me. I live on Facebook. I'll probably need therapy soon."

Jess shook her head. "That's sad," she said, laughing.

"No, what's sad is that you won't reach out to a classmate for some help."

Jess shrugged.

Melissa shook her head, and then pushed her chair back. "Do you want a refill?"

"I'm OK," Jess replied.

Melissa rose from her stool, walked around the island, and went to the other side of her large kitchen to refill her mug with the word *Diva* in bold letters printed on it.

Jess took a moment to glance around the kitchen, something she always did when she visited. Black marble countertops, stainless steel, state-of-the-art appliances, marble tiles, cherry-wood cabinets, all accentuated by rich sepia-colored walls and large windows giving way to an abundance of sunlight. It was a kitchen Jess would have loved to have had. And maybe had she not decided to quit school to focus on a modeling career that she never really had the dedication for, she could have gotten her degree, gotten a high-paying job in the media, and had what Melissa had. But, of course, had she gone down that road, there would have never been a happy-hour party to attend; she and Esias would have never met; and Jeanette and Jasmine wouldn't exist. Life as she knew it would not exist.

She smiled and let go of the fleeting *what-if* thought, and looked up at Melissa as she came back to the island big enough for four.

"So . . . since you mentioned the word *chat* . . . I'm curious . . . is that something you do often?"

"Only every time I'm on Facebook," Melissa said, sitting down.

"With friends or strangers?"

"Both. But more with strangers. Friends get on my nerves sometimes." Melissa laughed, then took a full sip of coffee.

Jess shook her head. "You're crazy!"

"Hey . . . I'm single and have no man at the moment."

"Still . . . with strangers?"

"Don't knock it till you've tried it, girlfriend."

"No, thanks. I have a husband to chat with."

Melissa drank some more coffee and hmmm'd over the rim of her mug. "How is Mr. Esias doing?" she asked, putting down her mug.

"He's good. Just busy."

"Anything close to happening with his music?"

"He's been working with some local rap group. He says he's got some really good tracks."

Melissa nodded. "Good. I can't wait to hear them. That's one talented man you have, and sooner or later, something's going to happen for him."

Jess gave a half smile and tried not to let it show that she'd been feeling as though later was going to come before sooner. She drank some of her coffee. "So, anyway . . . I still don't see how you can chat with strangers."

"It's just chatting, Jess."

"Still . . . there are a lot of predators out there."

"It's not like I'm sending them pictures or my address, girl. Calm down. It's just harmless conversation to pass the time."

"Still . . ."

"If you didn't have your sexy husband at home to keep you company, you'd be chatting too."

Jess shrugged. "I don't know. But I really doubt it."

"Trust me . . . you would."

Jess raised her eyebrows, took another swallow of coffee that was now lukewarm, and then looked at her watch. "I have to get going," she said, grabbing her purse. "I told Shirley I'd be there by seven to get the girls. Plus I have a seminar tonight."

Melissa smiled. "OK, but next time you visit, stop and get the girls first. I miss my godchildren."

Jess rose from her stool. "I will."

"I'm glad you came by. I miss seeing you."

Jess smiled. "I miss you too. It's just with work, the kids, school—"

"You don't have to explain anything to me, sis," Melissa said. "I'm proud of everything you're doing."

"Thanks. I'm proud of myself."

They hugged and planted kisses on each other's cheeks.

"Go and get your study on and reach out to one of your classmates," Melissa said as they walked to the front door.

Jess shook her head. "No, thanks. I'll leave the chatting to you."

A few minutes later, Jess sat in the front seat of her minivan and thought about her conversation with her best friend, particularly one thing Melissa had said. That she chatted but never sent out pictures to anyone.

She sighed and turned the key in the ignition, and as she pulled away from the curb, she looked at herself in her rearview mirror and said, "You're such a hypocrite."

Chapter 5

Wow! U r gorgeous.

Jess smiled. She had tried. On the drive from Melissa's to pick up the girls from aftercare. On the way home with the siblings arguing in the back. At home while she prepared dinner. As they ate, as the girls bathed afterward, after she tucked them in with good night kisses, and right before she logged into her seminar and the AOL instant messenger.

She had tried.

Told herself that she wasn't going to speak to Jayson anymore. Promised herself that she wasn't going to seek him out again, and that if he sent her a message, she wasn't going to respond. Things had gone too far. She'd gone too far. She had to put an end to it. She was married. She had a family. That's what was important. Work, family, school; she had no time for games she had no right playing in the first place.

So she had tried.

And before she could accept that she had failed miserably at trying, she typed, Thank u. Sorry I had 2 run out the way I did.

No aplgy needed. I knw why u had 2 go. It's cool.

Glad u weren't upset.

Not at all. The only thng I was, was speechless aftr I saw ur pic.

Jess felt her cheeks redden, and she looked down as though Jayson were standing in front of her and she

wanted to avoid his eyesight. Her conscience told her
to pay attention to the seminar and not Jayson's flattery. She needed to listen. She was falling behind again
as she focused less and less on her professor's voice
and instructions, and more on Jayson's words, which
she found herself eagerly waiting for more and more.

*Focus. You sent the picture, but it's not too late.
You can step off this broken path and go back to the
one leading you to safety. Don't respond. Close the
window. Exit out of the messenger. Focus on finishing
school. Not on a man who has no face.*

Keywords: no face.

Since sending her picture, she found herself wondering what Jayson looked like. It was another thing she
tried not to do, but she couldn't help it. He had a sexy
personality that came through in his messages and as
much as she didn't want to, she tried to put together an
image to match his words. Tall, short, fat, skinny, light,
dark; bald or with hair. He said he was a brotha with
no woman and no kids; he never stated his age though.
Could he be old?

What does it matter? her conscience chimed in. *You
don't need a face. A face makes him real, and you don't
need that. Log out of the messenger!*

Jess raised her head, cleared her throat, poised her
fingers over the keys of her laptop, and paused as her
heart began to race.

Do. Not. Make. Him. Real.

Heart thumping, heat inside of her rising, the sound
of the jazz playing softly from her iPod disappearing,
Jess typed: Thanks again. I don't get 2 say the same
thng though.

A moment of hesitation came. A moment in which
she could have chosen right over wrong. But that moment quickly passed when she hit Enter.

Seconds later, Jayson responded.

Wht do u mean?

I mean I don't hve a pic 2 admire.

I see. Is tht a dare 4 me?

Don't play, her conscience pleaded.

Maybe, Jess typed. I mean I did fulfill a dare 4 u.

Yes u did, and I'm apprctng ur beautiful eyes rght now.

Jess felt her cheeks redden again. Thank u

So is that my dare? U wnt a pic?

Jess cleared her throat and tried to deny the truth. Yes, she typed.

Wht kind of pic?

Loaded question, Jess typed, thinking of their last conversation.

Lol. I'm not scared.

Hmm.

Bring it.

Lol. Ur crazy!

So wht kind of pic?

Hmm . . . Same kind I sent u.

My face?

Yes.

OK. Wht's ur cell #?

Jess's heart was beating so heavily her body shook. *Crazy,* she thought. *Absolutely and positively insane.* It wasn't too late for her to get off of the ride. She'd stretched one foot across the line, but her other foot was still on the side of right, even if it was just barely settled on the tips of its toes. Still time to say never mind, to say that while she enjoyed their conversations, she couldn't go any further because it was wrong. Jess took a slow breath, and on a very extended exhale, sent her number to Jayson.

BRB.

OK.

Jess leaned forward in her chair, put her elbows on the edge of the dining table, and cradled her head in her hands. "You're crazy," she whispered. She closed her eyes and applied pressure to her temples with her palms as she began to furiously bounce on the toes of her right foot.

She thought about her husband. He had a tattoo on the outside of his left bicep. Words in black ink that read: Quiet Storm. They were words that described Esias's personality. On the outside he appeared easygoing and calm. He showed emotion, but never went overboard with his display. Those that didn't truly know him often described him as the one that never lost his cool. Mr. Even-Keeled. Only a select few ever saw the beast that lay dormant beneath Esias's composed exterior. A beast that when provoked, had the ability to lash out with a fury that would—and did—shock many.

Quiet storm.

If Esias knew what she'd done, what she was doing . . . A chill crept over her, the thought of his reaction, jarring.

Put the shoe on the other foot, her conscience said. *Put it there and imagine him doing this to you. Think about how you would feel.*

Jess ran her hands through her hair and sighed. She had to stop. She knew it. She pressed her lips together firmly and frowned as she pulled her head back away from her hands and made a move to click out of the messenger, when her cell phone chimed in the special way, alerting her that picture mail had come through.

For the briefest of moments, she stared at her phone before grabbing it to press a button to stop the chime, which at that moment seemed loud enough to clue her neighbors in on her indiscretion. Her heart, which had already been beating at a rapid, heavy pace, went into overdrive.

Truth or dare. A game she hadn't played since her teenage years. A game she had no business playing now.

Jess swallowed saliva, pressed the OK button to open the mail, and then looked at the picture of a man that belonged on the cover of *Ebony* magazine.

"Oh my."

She looked from side to side as though someone other than her sleeping girls were around to hear her, and then looked back down at the now very real Jayson Winston. Dark chocolate, with deep-set eyes that appeared to be looking through her. Full, pink-hued lips—lips that she could tell knew how to be used—framed by a full, but well-groomed goatee. High cheekbones, a strong nose untouched from the throes of battle, a muscular jaw. The coup de grâce, a Maxwell-type hairstyle, before Maxwell cut it all off.

Jess stared at Jayson with her mouth partly open. He looked to be in his late twenties to early thirties, and although he had captured himself from the shoulders up, it was obvious to her that Jayson took very good care of his body.

"Lord."

She looked over to her laptop screen. The words, Still thre? Or did I scare u away? were waiting for her.

She shook her head, looked at his photograph again, thought about how much better he must look in person, and then typed a response. Still here. And no, u defntly did not scare me away.

Good 2 knw.

Ur an . . . Jess paused and thought about the safest word to use: attractive man, she finished.

Thank u.

And u hve no wife? No girlfriend?

Nope.

And ur sure u don't hve a boyfriend either.

Told u, I don't swing on the opp side of the ballpark.

Lol. OK.

So . . . now we both hve faces 2 go wth the names.

Yes, we do.

What's nxt?

Jess gave the question some thought, and then answered as honestly as she could, I don't knw. I've never done anything like this bfre.

Nethr hve I.

I find tht hard 2 believe.

U do? Why?

I don't knw . . . u seem like a pro at this sort of thing.

No. I'm def not.

Mmm-hmm Jess typed, pulling the corner of her mouth back and rolling her eyes.

Seriously. I don't do ths kind of thing at all. I'm not a chatter.

OK. So wht made u reach out 2 me?

I don' t knw.

Mmm-hmm.

4 real. The best explntion I can gve is tht I saw ur name and sort of felt . . . complld 2 reach out.

Compelld? Interesting choice of word.

Most honest word I cld think of.

Compelld?

Compelld. U clled out to me. I reached. And then aftr I saw ur pic . . .

Jayson stopped typing, prompting Jess to probe. Aftr my picture . . . wht?

Sure u wnt me 2 go on?

Aftr my picture . . . wht?

Aftr ur pic . . . I got sucked in.

Jess smiled, looked at his picture again, and licked her lips. I see.

So?

So?

So . . . wht's nxt?

I really don't knw. U tell me. Ur the pro that started ths.

Lol. True. Well . . . technically, since I cmpltd ur dare, it's now my turn to ask u to choose again.

Hmm, Jess typed with a sneaky smile.

Truth or dare?

Jess's smile widened. This was so wrong. So very, very wrong. Yet, as wrong as it was, she couldn't deny the fact that it felt good, and perhaps that was because it was so wrong.

She and Esias had a good relationship, but everything had become so routine. Wake up, get themselves and the girls dressed, leave, drop them off to school or daycare, go to work, put in long hours, leave work, get the girls, go home, fix and eat dinner, give baths, tuck them in bed, go on the laptop for school, go to bed, sleep, and then wake up and do it all over again. Pecks on the lips between her and Esias occurred in the mornings before parting ways for work, and again in the evenings when they saw each other. Sex happened once, sometimes twice a month. They had the usual stressors any marriage had, but they weren't unhappy. They were just stuck, waddling through a muck that never changed.

Routine.

Talking to Jayson, doing what she was doing, had no place in the life she had, but the fact of the matter was Jess hadn't felt this alive in a long time. Jayson said she'd left him speechless. She couldn't remember the last time she'd had that effect on someone. Was he lying about not chatting with anyone else, about not sending photographs? Maybe. He did appear to be up front about the things he said. At least so far. But, of course, maybe not was also a possibility. But as she glanced at his picture again, she surmised that lying or not, she didn't care.

Battle lost, her conscience fell silent.

She typed, Truth.

Chapter 6

Truth or dare?

Truth.

Do u evr think abt, or hve u evr been tempted 2 not b so safe with ur qstns and dares? B honst.

Jess looked at the question on her screen and bit down on her bottom lip as she thought about how to respond to Jayson's question. Had she thought about not being safe?

Had she refrained from asking him another dare because for the past week whenever she'd taken a glance at his picture, she wondered just what it would be like seeing more of him? Had she been playing it safe because the more she found herself looking at him, the more tempted she became to dare him to send another picture showing her just a little more?

Truth or dare.

Playing it safe had never been part of the game when she was a teenager. It was never fun that way. Being bold, daring—*that* was fun; *that* was why you played. *That* was the only reason for playing. Jess looked at Jayson's question. He wanted her to be honest. It was, after all, a requirement. Safe. She thought about it, and as she did, a word came to her mind: Desire.

She took a breath, poised her fingers above the keys of her laptop, exhaled, and typed.

Maybe.

Maybe? Interesting.

Hve u? Jess asked.

U wnt the truth?

Of course.

But can u handle the truth?

Lol! Just answr!

I've been tempted evr since I saw ur pic.

Bumps rose along Jess's arms. Hve you? she replied.

W/out qstn.

How tempted?

Extrmly. So tempted tht I almost gave in.

Hmm . . . I see.

Do u?

I do. What kept u frm asking? Were u scared?

Ha! Tht's funny.

What's so funny abt tht? U said u've been tempted 2 not b safe, yet u always playd it tht way. I figure u must b scared.

Jess . . . believe me when I say ths . . . my playng it safe was more 4 ur benefit.

Mine?

Most defntly. I didn't wnt 2 offend u in any way.

Offended? Why do u think I wld b?

I can b bold, Jess. With qstns and dares.

So?

U might not b ready 4 it.

I'm grwn.

Hmm.

So?

So.

So give me a bold question. I dare u.

Lol. That's a dangerous dare, sexy. And yes, I did say sexy.

TY.

Jess smiled and nibbled down on her bottom lip again. A few days ago her conscience would have been screaming at her, demanding that she cease with the foolishness, that she come to her senses and grow the hell up. But that was a few days ago when she'd been in her right mind; when the voice of rationality was far louder and stronger than that of irresponsibility.

A few days ago, hell . . . a few weeks ago, she would have never thought she'd be eagerly waiting and wanting to refrain from holding back with a man that wasn't her husband. Of course, the more she thought about it, the more she realized that holding back with Esias was all she had been doing.

She typed, So . . . I'm waiting.

I'm thnkng.

Thnkng? I thought u said u were bold.

Tht's the prblm. I want to ease u in, so I have 2 b gentle with the 1st qstn.

Gentle? Who told u I like it that way?

Hmm . . . so rough is ur prfrnce?

Jess felt a tingle in between her legs.

Gentle is nice, but rough can b . . . powerfully pleasing.

I see. Powerfully pleasing. That's a hell of an answer.

Was it 2 bold 4 u?

Lol. Not even close.

My turn.

OK. Let's see what u got.

Boy . . . ur askng 4 it.

Lol! Yes I am.

Another gush in between her legs. She grabbed her cell phone, which sat in its usual position off to her side, and pushed one of the buttons, waking it from the sleep mode it had been in. As it did, Jayson's tantalizing image appeared. She licked her lips. What r u lookng 4 exactly? she typed with one hand.

What r u willng 2 give?

Jess's heart was beating heavily from the excitement of the very wrong thing that was going on. Tht depends, she answered.

On?

On how much u can tke.

O I can tke a lot, Jess. The real qstn is how much can u gve?

Let's just say as dormant as things hve been lately . . . I hve an overabundance in the well.

Hmm. Filled 2 the point of ovrflowng?

Right now . . . it's tricklng over.

Wow.

Jess laughed out loud. The sudden outburst caught her by surprise. She quickly clamped her hand over her mouth.

"Jess?"

"Dammit," she whispered.

She frowned, powered her phone down, and before answering her husband, who'd just called out to her from upstairs, she quickly typed a message to Jayson.

Hve 2 go. We'll continue later. In the meantime, I dare u 2 send me a bolder pic.

She exited out of messenger. She was supposed to be up late trying to remain on solid ground after having finally gotten caught up in her classes. "Yes?"

"It's late," Esias said. "Are you planning on getting any sleep?"

Jess wanted to go off and tell him to leave her alone and to go back to bed, but how could she when a reaction like that was one he didn't deserve? She sighed and said, "I was just shutting things down." She took a glance at her cell. She'd dared Jayson for more. She couldn't believe it. It was so wrong, but as she shut down her laptop, got up from her chair, clicked off the lights in the dining room, she went to bed eager to see what picture would be waiting for her when she awoke.

Chapter 7

Jayson stood stone still as one word came to his mind.
Kismet. The way he and Jess met. The ease with which
their conversation flowed. The natural progression
they'd made. Kismet, meant to be, destiny, soul mates;
no matter how you said it, the fact of the matter was he
and Jess were perfect for each other. Jayson knew it and
felt it in his bones.

Jess knew it too. That's why she wanted a bolder picture. She wanted to see what she couldn't stop thinking
about. She wanted to gaze at what she wanted to feel;
what she yearned for when they spoke. She was starv-
ing and wanted to taste what her stomach growled for.
Jayson knew it because he wanted all of those things
too. He knew it because they were of like mind.

Kismet.

The hairs on his arms rose as his blood flowed and
his dick became erect. He'd never felt the connection
with the others. He'd never experienced anything so
symbiotic. It was powerful, stirring. Without having
even consummated their inevitable union, it was sexually thrilling on a level he'd begun to think was impossible to achieve. "Jess," he whispered. "Jessie. Jessica.
Jesssssss."

He smiled while his manhood bounced. He put his
right hand around his tip and sucked in a short breath.
His hands were like ice against his hot skin. He slid his
hand down to his shaft and squeezed. Blood pumped

rhythmically beneath his palm, the way he wanted to move inside of Jess. In. Out. In. Out. In. Out. Slowly, methodically like Prince's classically penned ode to a one-time sexual encounter, "Darling Nikki."

In. Out.

Back. Forth.

Clockwise. Counterclockwise.

Each thrust deeper than the one before it. Deep enough to hit her core, to reach her soul.

"Jess," he sang in a whisper again. "My Jess."

Jayson squeezed his shaft harder, making his tip balloon, and reached for his cell phone in front of him. Jess wanted a bolder picture. He smiled again, set his cell to camera mode, held it up at arm's length at an angle off to his left, to capture his good side. He stared into the lens of his 2.0 mega pixelated camera. His expression was serious, intense, and ruggedly seductive. "Come and get this." He said that with his eyes, with the setting of his jaw. He squeezed harder on his manhood, and as he did, he pressed the button to capture the bolder picture Jess dared him for.

And then he heard moaning.

He stepped out of the bathroom he'd been standing in. It wasn't his bathroom. It belonged to Rita. She was in his Visual Basics class. She'd wanted him to come and visit her when her husband went away for his weeklong business meeting in New York. Plans had been made for a month now. She lay spread eagle on her bed, naked.

Jayson walked over to her, his dick bouncing with each step. She moaned again. Jayson grinned. "You want more, don't you?"

He sat down on the edge of the bed beside her at her waist and traced his index finger along the length of her thigh. "Are you comfortable? I didn't tie you up too tightly, did I?"

He ran his hand down from the middle of her thigh, past her knee, and made his way to her left ankle, which he'd bound to one of the four bedposts with rope. He pulled on the binding, then, satisfied with the job he'd done, stretched to her other ankle, checked the binding there as well, and then reached up and checked the bindings around each wrist holding her to the bedposts as well.

Rita whimpered and Jayson looked at her. Tears were falling from her swollen, red eyes as she trembled. Blood was trickling down from her nostril; the result of a slap he'd had to give her when she tried to resist what she'd told him she wanted over and over again in their numerous and very explicit chats.

Jayson didn't like hitting women. It was something his father used to do to his mother, and he hated that. But he'd had to hit her. He had to calm her down. He caressed her cheek, and as he did, his fingers grazed over duct tape he had pressed down over her mouth.

"Do you want it again?" he asked. "Is that why you're crying? Because it was so good?" Rita moaned beneath the tape. Jayson grinned. "OK . . . I'll give it to you again. I'll fuck you the way you love to be fucked." Jayson smiled thinly while Rita moaned as tears cascaded down her cheeks.

Rita's husband was away on business, but he wasn't the breadwinner of the family. Rita was with the make-up company she'd started. A company that was worth millions. She had offered Jayson money before he covered her mouth. However much he had wanted, it was his. Just let her go. Jayson had turned the money down though. He wasn't there for the money. He was there to complete the game they played. It was why he'd flown to California.

Jayson climbed on top of her. He would fuck her again and again just like she'd dared him to, and then he would leave, knowing that she would never utter a word of his existence to anyone, because he had pictures and chat messages in his phone, and Rita's reputation was everything to her.

Chapter 8

So did u see the pic?

Jess's vagina pulsated. *Had she seen the picture?* She licked her lips, and as she did, her thoughts went back to the moment when, two minutes after she had turned on her cell phone, Jayson's picture came through. She'd been driving, taking the girls to day care before going into work, and had nearly rear-ended an Infiniti Coupe, as she'd found it nearly impossible to look away from the fulfillment on her dare Jayson had sent.

Shirtless from just centimeters above where his penis resided, Jayson was a physical specimen the likes of which she'd only seen in videos and magazines. His shoulders were round, hard, well-defined. His chest was thick and cut. His abdominals rippled and came in three exquisitely defined sets of two's.

The picture had her mouth hanging open and had stolen her breath away, and only because of a blaring car horn and a near accident one lane over did she look up in time to see that if she didn't slam down on the brakes of her Camry, she was going to cause severe damage to the rear of the Infiniti and the front of her car. Her heart pounded as her daughters screamed and the scent of burnt rubber from her tires wafted in through her opened windows, but it didn't pound from the near collision.

Jayson's picture.

That's what had her heart racing. That's what had her palms getting slick with perspiration. Bolder is what she'd dared him to provide. As traffic began to move at a snail's pace, she struggled to not focus for more than a few seconds at a time at the much-bolder picture Jayson had sent.

Had she seen the picture?

During the rest of the drive to drop off the girls, all day at work and afterward when she picked up the girls and headed home, that's all she had seen and thought about. She'd spent the entire day on autopilot, doing what she'd become programmed to do.

She pressed the button on her cell phone, waking it from its slumber and smiled as Jayson looked back at her from the screen on her cell. *Had she seen his picture?*

Pulsating in her panties, she typed, Yes, I did.

And were u disapointd?

Jess looked from his words to his eyes, to his lips, to the small dark nipples on his chest, and shook her head. Not at all.

Whew! I was worried.

Worried? Why? U have a very sexy . . .

Jess paused, took a breath, and released it slowly as she felt herself becoming warm. *Calm down*, she thought. She hit the backspace key several times, and then began typing again.

. . . hve a nice body.

TY.

Ur welcome.

So . . . it wasn't 2 bold? Was worried abt offending u.

Jess looked back at his picture and went from the chest to the seams in his abdominals, and then down to where her imagination took over. *More.* The word ran through her mind.

She shook her head again, ran her hand from her neck to the top of her breasts, which were loose beneath her tank top without the confinement of her bra.

I told you I'm a big girl. It wld tke a lot more than tht 2 offend me.

Is that so? That sounds like a challenge.

Do u want 2 offend me?

Not at all. Just curious 2 know what it wld take.

R u?

Very.

I see. Well, I can tell u tht it wld tke a lot.

Hmm.

Lol. Ur funny.

So ur sure u liked wht u saw?

Jess raised her eyebrows and grinned. I did.

Wht was the 1st thought tht came to ur mind whn u saw it?

Jess put the tip of her index finger in her mouth and bit down on her nail softly as her lips spread into a sneaky smile.

How much weight can those shoulders bear?

How hard are your muscles? How soft?

How hard do your nipples get?

How smooth is each ripple in your abs?

What does it look like beneath the bottom edge of the photograph?

These were the first thoughts that ran through her mind all at the same time. She took a breath and released it with a "humph," and typed, Tht u care abt ur body.

TY. I try 2.

"You're doing more than trying, baby," Jess whispered.

So ... u askd 4 bolder. Did I meet the rquirmnt?

Jess chuckled. I guess so.

I aim 2 please.

Hmm. It's always nice whn a man aims high.

I'm an expert marksman.

R u?

Bulls eye evrytme.

Interesting.

So . . .

So?

Unless ur backng out, it's my turn 2 ask.

Jess nodded to herself. She'd thought of this during the day. Her turn. Her truth or dare. Her choice. If she so chose.

Yes, it is.

R u bckng out?

I'm not a quitter.

Thn in tht case . . . Truth or dare?

Jess's heart thumped, and as it did, the voice of reason resurfaced again, only this time, instead of pleading and begging that she cease with the game entirely, it presented her with a compromise.

If you're going to play—fine—then play. But at least be smart and safe about it. No dares no matter what! Can you just do that? Can you just be smart and safe?

Jess looked down at her cell, reached out, hit a button and brought Jayson's picture back to life again. She'd been selfish. She hadn't given him the option of truth.

She took another breath.

Her voice of reason began to fade away.

She exhaled and chose. Dare.

R u sure?

Jess swallowed saliva. Yes.

Ur not scared?

I told u I'm grwn.

OK. Jst mkng sure.

So wht's my dare?
Hmm . . . I wnt a pic. A bolder pic.
Copycat.
LOL!
Wht do u want 2 see?
Ur breasts.

Jess felt her nipples harden beneath the cotton of her top. The voice of reason's volume rose again like steam.

Don't do it! Don't play this way! Be smart! You don't want to regret this!

Jess slid her hand beneath her shirt and laid it flat against her belly. Her breasts. He wanted to see them.

Back out now before it's too late! No dares!

She began to trail her hand upward like a snake. Slow, deliberate. Her conscience pleaded with her again, but as it did, each word grew softer.

Her breasts. They hadn't been seen by anyone other than her daughters, Esias, and her gynecologist.

Her hand went up, cupped her left breast, and as it did, she took in a breath. She'd touched herself before; innocently in the shower, in front of the mirror doing her self-breast exam, massaging them at the end of long days after removing her bra. She'd touched them for pleasure too, when the urge hit and either Esias wasn't home or in the mood to provide a release. She'd squeezed them. She'd closed her eyes and leaned her head back and ran her fingers over and around her nipples.

But not like she was doing now, staring at Jayson as he stared back at her with his shirt off, his muscles bulging. His manhood . . .

Jess moaned as she enjoyed the feel of her C-cup enveloped in her palm while her index finger and thumb pinched her nipple hard. She moaned as a tingling sensation ran through her. *His manhood*, she thought.

What had it been doing below the border? She moaned again and tried to imagine what it must have looked like. Had it been hard like his muscles? Had it been swollen?

She grabbed her cell and reluctantly made Jayson's handsome face disappear as she switched it to camera mode. She didn't want to, but she let go of her breast, took a quick look to her right toward the staircase leading upstairs, and listened for footsteps. Esias wasn't home, but her oldest liked to be in other people's business and knew how to tread lightly. She listened for creaks and shuffles, and when she was satisfied that her daughter was still in bed, she hiked her tank top up over her head, leaned back in the chair and turned her camera toward her. She palmed her breast again, squeezed her nipple to make it stand out even more than it still was, and looked into the camera lens.

Can't believe I'm doing this, she thought.

Can't believe I want to.

She looked at Jayson through the lens, licked her lips, offered her breast up for a snack, and took a series of six photographs. When she was finished, she put her cell down and quickly put her shirt back on. She was breathing heavily. Panting, from the erotic thrill she'd just experienced. Her shirt back on, she looked at her laptop. Jayson had been looking for her.

R u thre? Did I scare u away? Jess?

Jess sat forward and typed.

Sorry. Yes. I'm here.

O OK. Is evrythng OK?

Yes.

OK. Good.

I took the pic.

U did?

Yes.

Wow!

Gve me a minute 2 send thm 2 u.

OK!

But . . .

But?

After I send thm, I'm logging off.

U r? why?

Jess felt the heat in her cheeks rise. She'd taken the pictures and had enjoyed doing it, but for some reason, she was embarrassed about what his reaction was going to be.

My husband just came home. He's outside tlking 2 a neighbor.

O, OK. L

Gng 2 send it in 2 minutes. I'll talk 2 u tmrrw.

OK.

Nght.

Nght, sexy.

Jess smiled. Esias hadn't called her that in a long while. She logged out of the messenger, then grabbed her cell and scrolled through the pictures she'd taken. She'd captured the angle almost perfectly and had hidden some of the weight around her middle. Jayson had called her sexy, and in each of the six shots, the word applied. She settled on two of them, then typed in Jayson's cell number and hit Send.

Her dare was done. She'd gone bolder. It would be Jayson's turn next.

Chapter 9

It was time to take things to the next level.

Jayson worked his jaw and stared at Jess's breasts, at her nipples. Small, round, coffee-colored, hard. He gnawed on a piece of skin hanging from his bottom lip as his manhood jumped beneath his boxers. "Perfect," he whispered, his eyes fixated on her picture. Full round breasts with just a slight childbearing, breast-feeding sag to them.

After childbirth, particularly two births, a woman's body changed. Her hips tended to spread, her waistline lost the hourglass shape, her thighs grew larger, the stomach poked out farther, and of course, her breasts dropped. Because of these changes, her self-esteem lowered. Many women didn't feel attractive anymore, didn't feel desired. They existed without any real identity. "Mommy" is all they were, and nothing more.

Jayson liked the sag. He liked the pouch, the broader hips. To him, the change in a woman's body gave her more character. It gave her validation as a "real" woman. He chose the majority of the women he did for that reason first. Reason number two was because women that had children gave more than those who didn't. All they needed was to feel wanted. Make a mommy feel like a "mami" and she would do things a lot of women without kids weren't willing to do without getting something in return. She would chat with strangers, send pictures, agree to meetings with promised ecstasy in the back of tinted vehicles in front of their homes, and agree to be fucked in their beds when their husbands were away.

Jayson smiled while his manhood pulsed and begged to be released. He stared at Jess's perfect breasts—C-cup he was sure. The time had definitely come.

Jess was ready.

So was he.

He'd finally found her, and he didn't want to let another second of wasted time go by.

"Jess and Jayson sitting in a tree . . ."

His dick jumped in tune to the rhythm of the nursery rhyme. *Next conversation*, he promised. During their next chat, he and Jess would move on with their natural progression of eventual and destined bliss.

He looked at Jess as she stared at him with her breast in her hand. The yearning in her eyes was powerful, intense, and high. Most of all, it was filled with hunger.

"Soon, sexy," Jayson said, lowering his boxers. "Soon all of your needs will be met, and you'll never have to go without again. Neither will I."

Chapter 10

Alisa sat on the edge of her bed hugging herself while tears fell hard and fast. "Oh God," she whispered, wiping tears away, her attempts futile. She leaned forward and hugged herself harder. "How could I have let this happen?"

She shook her head and cursed herself for being so gullible. She knew better. She'd fallen for the okeydoke before, but she was younger, more naïve then. She was older now, wiser, schooled; this shouldn't have happened. She should have recognized the signs. But there hadn't been any signs, had there? There hadn't been any indication that Jayson Winston had been anything other than what he'd professed to be: a male version of her, neglected, in need of attention and affection. In need of passion and romance.

In all of their chats, Alisa had never suspected that their understanding of each other hadn't been real. She'd believed him when he told her that he had never felt so connected with anyone before. She'd agreed when he said there was something "right" about them. "Kismet," he had called it. "Destiny."

Alisa had felt the connection, the ease. In twelve years of marriage, she hadn't experienced that, but in a matter of a few weeks, she did with Jayson, who adored her and wanted to satisfy her mentally, physically, and emotionally, because she deserved nothing less. They couldn't divorce their spouses because of their families, but they could make a vow to be each other's one and only. Jayson wanted that. He said he would be married legally on paper to his wife, but spiritually, it would be to Alisa where his heart would go.

Tears dropped harder from Alisa's eyes. She was such a fool. Pictures, texts, chats, now pregnancy. And just as swiftly as Jayson had come into her life, he was now gone, and had been since she'd done all of the uninhibited things with him that she'd promised to do fifteen weeks ago.

Pregnant. She'd been safe and smart by making sure Jayson had used protection. So how could this have happened?

Alisa cried. Four months prior, her husband had gotten a vasectomy because with four children, all boys, he didn't want any more. Now she was two months pregnant and only within the last month did she miss a period. Alisa shivered and cursed herself for ever responding to Jayson Winston's initial chat message.

Chapter 11

"So how is the class going?"

Jess looked over at her husband. He was sitting on the couch, a plate of rice and chicken in his hand, a Heineken beer bottle on the coffee table in front of him. He was watching TV. ESPN, the U.S. Open, a match between Serena Williams and Maria Sharapova, two of his favorites.

Esias was in his usual nighttime attire—a pair of shorts, a wife beater, and no socks. His ankles were in need of lotion. He was supposed to have been at the studio, but he'd said he was tired and wanted to just come home and relax and spend time with the girls. He also missed spending time with his wife.

Four weeks ago, Jess wouldn't have had a problem with him sitting in the middle of their brown leather couch, but a lot had changed and four weeks ago was a long time in the past, and now instead of looking at her husband with a soft, appreciative gaze of love and yearning, she stared at him with a glare as hard as steel.

Her tone low, her voice tight, she said, "Fine." She added nothing more.

Esias shoveled a forkful of rice into his mouth, chewed, and then swallowed it down along with a sip of his beer. "Is the class getting any easier?"

Jess exhaled, then pulled in the corners of her mouth as she frowned. "No," she said. "But, whatever."

"Whatever?" Esias asked with a cocked eyebrow. "What do you mean, 'whatever'?"

Jess exhaled heavily again. "Whatever means whatever, Esias."

His fork filled and halfway up toward his mouth, he paused and looked at her. "What's with the attitude?"

"What attitude?"

"You're acting like I did something to you."

Jess rolled her eyes. "I don't have an attitude," she said. "I'm just trying to study."

"I understand that. I was just wondering how things were going."

"And I told you."

"Yeah . . . with an attitude."

Jess rolled her eyes again and stole a glance down at the time on her laptop. 9:50. In ten minutes, her seminar for her PHP class would be beginning. That meant that in ten minutes Jayson would be sending her a message. In the four weeks since they'd been chatting, Esias had either not been home, or he'd been upstairs sleeping. Tonight, he was on the couch, upsetting her flow.

She shook her head. "I told you I don't have an attitude."

Esias took another swallow of Heineken. "Bullshit," he said.

Jess released a frustrated exhale. "I'm in danger of failing my class, Esias. Neither the professor, nor the textbooks are any help. I've tried attending the tutoring session with nothing to show for it. I'm frustrated."

"I get that, but you don't need to let it out on me."

Jess gave a one-sided smile of irritation. "OK, Esias. You're right. Can I go back to focusing now?"

"Sure, Jess. Sure. Give me shit for asking how your classes were."

Jess pulled the corners of her mouth back again and stole another glance at the time. 9:56. Her heart began to thump. "I still don't see why you didn't go to the studio."

"Is it a crime that I didn't?"

"No. I just thought you were trying to get the CD done. Didn't you say you had some people interested in it?"

"I do. But like I said earlier, I was tired and needed a break, and I wanted to spend some time with the girls before they went to bed. I also wanted to try to spend some time at least being around you. Between work, the studio, your job, and your classes, we barely see each other anymore."

Jess shrugged and said, unapologetically, "Priorities."

"So what . . . are you saying, I'm neglecting mine?"

Jess huffed and looked at the time again. One minute to go. "I'm just saying you have someone interested in your work. Maybe taking a night off wasn't the best thing to do."

"I don't think one night will kill me, Jess."

"A lot can happen in one night," Jess replied, her thoughts on her first night with Jayson.

Esias put his plate down so hard on the coffee table, his fork jumped and fell to the hardwood floor. "What the hell? I took one goddamned night off to relax with my family. I don't need a fucking lecture."

"I'm not lecturing you, Esias."

"The hell you're not!"

Jess sighed as the time on her clock read 10:00. She looked at her cell phone, where Jayson's picture sat waiting for her to glance at. Tonight she'd planned on giving him a dare to match her own. Tonight, without Esias there to harass her.

"Look," she said, her tone conceding defeat in a war she didn't want. "I don't have the time or desire to argue. My seminar is about to start. I'm going upstairs." She began to gather her books, preparing to get out of her chair.

"No," Esias said, grabbing the remote. He clicked the TV off and tossed the remote to the corner of the couch. "I'll take care of my *priorities*," he said, making quotation marks with his fingers, "and just go to the goddamned studio." He grabbed his plate, his beer, and went to the kitchen and slammed them down on the countertop.

When he stormed off upstairs, Jess released a breath she had been holding at the tail end of their argument. Jayson had sent her a message.

Hey, sexy. R u there?

She took a glance toward the staircase, and then replied, Esias is here. But he's leaving soon.

OK. I luvd ur pic.

Jess felt the heat in her cheeks as she smiled.

Did u?

Uh-huh. U lookd like u were hvng fun.

Jess's smile grew wider. Lol. I was. All alone.

That's a shame.

A door slammed shut upstairs, and seconds later, footsteps thudded down the staircase.

Jess shut her messenger down quickly, raised the volume so that her professor's voice could be heard clearly, and looked up as Esias walked into the dining room.

"I'll see you after I've taken care of my *priorities*."

Jess frowned. "Whatever, Esias. I didn't tell you to go anywhere."

"Yeah, OK," Esias said. He turned and without a good-bye, walked out of the house, slamming the door shut behind him.

Jess wanted to bring up the messenger again without hesitation, but she waited for Esias's Camry to start, and then pull away from in front of their home. When it did, she logged back in and typed, I'm bck.

Chapter 12

Jayson smiled.

She was back. Back and ready. Tonight was the night. Electricity ran through him to the tips of his nerve endings. Their relationship was going to move on to the next level. All she had to do was give him the dare he knew she was going to give.

Jess.

She was so right for him.

He typed, U were gone 2 lng. I missed u.

That would make her smile, he knew, because he knew her.

Sorry. I was jst waitng 4 him 2 go.

And he is now?

Yes.

And ur grls?

Sleeping. They're wiped out.

I bet ur grls r cuties.

I wn't lie. Thy r!

Lol. Thy get it frm their momma.

Flattery will get you everywhere.

Jayson ran his tongue across the inside of his upper lip. *So ready,* he thought. It was time. He grabbed his cell, pressed a button, and Jess's breasts filled the screen. They were his wallpaper. He couldn't get enough of them.

His manhood came to life. *Time,* he thought again.

He typed, I'm lookng at ur pic rght now.

R u?

I can't stop lookng at it.

Really? What was ur first thght when u saw it?

1st thght?

Yes.

Sure u wnt 2 knw? It's a bold thght.

Tell me!

OK. 1st thght . . . tht I wsh my tongue was circlng around ur nipples.

Jayson looked at his cell phone, his dick erect, and imagined Jess's breasts in his hands and mouth. He could feel them. Smooth, soft, her nipples hard beneath the tips of his fingers. His dick throbbed. It could feel them too.

Was tht 2 bold?

No. Not at all.

U hve some of the most engaging breasts I've evr seen.

TY.

I wld kiss and caress the hell out of thm. I wld adore thm.

Mmm. They haven't been adored in a long time. Squeezed and fondled yes, but not adored. Tht would b nice.

That's a real shame. Breasts like tht, nipples as prfctly shaped as urs shld b caressed gently the way u wld handle a newborn. Thn thy shld be kissd, lickd, pinchd sftly, slwly. Thy shld b savored.

Jayson stared at Jess's picture, at her hard nipples. Nipples that he knew were harder now. She was wet and dripping from the things he'd just said. There was no doubt in his mind.

Mmm. Tht wld b so nice.

I wld hold, kiss, and admire thm for hrs, Jess. U wldn't b able 2 say thy were neglctd evr again.

Wow. Tht sounds so good.

Touch thm 4 me, Jess. I luvd the way u held thm in ur hand. It made me so hard.

A few long seconds passed before Jess responded.

Mmm.

Squeeze ur prfct nipples 4 me.

I luv to hve thm squeezed hard.

I wld do tht rght now if I cld. I wld pinch and twist thm bfre I took thm in my mouth.

Mmm. God, Jayson. I'm ... I'm ...

Ur wht, Jess?

I'm so horny.

R u wet?

Very.

Jayson smiled.

Her hands were on her pussy now. He could all but see it.

How wet?

Flooding.

Wow. Wish I cld taste u. Do u like to be tasted?

Of course!

I wld so do tht 2 u.

Mmm. My husband never goes down on me.

Wht?? Ur hubby's a fool. I wld savor and adore ur breasts and drnk evry drop ur pussy had to offr.

I give, but haven't gotten in such a lng time.

If I were thre, I wld drink u rght now.

Every drop?

Evry drop. U'd b dry by the time I'd b done wth u.

Mmmmmm.

Time, Jayson thought as his manhood jumped. *The time was now, the time had come.*

U still owe me a dare.

J Yes, I do.

R u ready 2 gve I?

Yes!

The corners of Jayson's mouth rose. He switched his cell phone to camera mode, leaned back in his chair, and pointed it at his cock. As always, he was sitting naked, sweat running down the small of his back.

I'm waitng. *Ask for what you want, my love.*

R u still hard?

Jayson's blood pumped. I am.

How hard?

Like steel.

Prove it.

Jayson angled his call to the right angle above his dick. And how do u wnt me 2 prove it?

A pic. I wnt a pic.

Of wht?

U knw.

R u afrd 2 tell me wht u wnt?

No.

So thn, if ur so grwn like u always say, thn tell me wht u wnt 2 see.

OK, fine. I'm not scared.

Prove it.

I will.

I'm waitng.

I wnt a picture of ur dick.

Is tht a dare?

Yes.

Hmm. And ur sure u wnt to see tht?

Very sure.

Jayson smiled, and as he did, he pressed the OK button and captured the proof Jess desired. *Time,* he thought once more. OK, I hve it. R u ready 4 it?

Yes.

OK. Sendng now, but . . .

But?

I wnt an instant reaction.

Instant reaction? Wht do u mean?

I mean I don't wnt u running away again. As soon as
u see the pic, I want 2 know ur thghts. OK?

OK.

Coming now.

Jayson hit the button to send his picture and as he
did, a new chat message appeared in the upper left corner of his screen. He drew his lips together and shook
his head. It was Rita from his Visual Basics class. He
had fucked her, and then left her spread eagle on her
bed, her wrists and ankles still tied to her bedposts. He
had fucked her hard and deep. She'd cried and moaned
behind the duct tape over her mouth when he pounded
her, and the sounds of her whimpering had made his
blood pump harder. He looked at her message. This
one started the same as the previous three he had ignored since leaving her.

U raped me u son of a bitch!

Jayson sighed. It was time to be rid of her for good.

I gave u wht u wntd, Rita.

I wntd 2 b fckd not tied and gagged!

It made the exprence more exctng, don't u thnk?

Ur an asshole!!!

Jayson laughed.

And ur an unfaithful whore

Fck u! I'm gng 2 the police!

2 tell thm wht, Rita? That u fckd around on ur hsbnd?

No! 2 tell thm that u raped me!

I did wht u dared me 2 do. Do u wnt me 2 send u
the trnscrpts of our conversations 2 hlp u rmembr? Or
bettr yet, I'll just keep thm 4 the police, ur famly and
the 676 Facebook friends tht u hve.

Jess's minimized messenger window began to flash
orange at the bottom of his screen, indicating that she
had responded. Good-bye, Rita.

Ur a bastard, Jayson!!

Jayson smiled.

Truth or dare, Rita. U playd. I won. Game ovr. Now . . . don't send me anymore mssgs or everyone is going 2 knw a lot mre abt u than thy do now.

I hate u!!! I hope u die!!!

Jayson laughed and closed Rita's chat window. Just like the others, her threats meant nothing to him. Their lives were locked away in folders with their names attached in his e-mail and in the memory card of his cell. They could go to the police if they wanted to, but if they did, two things would happen. One—he would air their dirty laundry out for everyone to see. And two—nothing would ever happen to him because Jayson Winston didn't exist.

"I dare you, Rita," he said, then he maximized Jess's window and smiled as capital letters with exclamation points at the end greeted him.

O my!!

Do u like?

It was an unnecessary question, but he liked to read their responses.

I . . . I . . . Wow! I do.

R u sure? Don't be afrd 2 hurt my feelngs.

Jayson . . . ur so big and thick.

It looks better in person.

Mmm. I hve no doubt that it does.

I'm throbbing just knwng that ur lookng at it rght now. U r still lookng at it, aren't u?

I am. I can't stop lookng at it.

Tht's how I am wth ur breasts. I'm staring at thm just imagining how they must feel.

Mmm. I'm doing the same thing.

I strokd looking at ur pic, Jess. I strokd and I came.

Did u cum a lot?

More thn a lot.

Mmm. Just imagining tht is makng me wet.

Wnt 2 taste u bad.

Wld u really?

Wthout hesitation.

That sounds so good.

Jayson nodded as he ran his hands up and down the length of his shaft. *Of course it does*, he thought.

It wld feel good, Jess.

Mmm. Wld it?

Bettr thn good.

I need tht. 2 feel good.

Ur a beautiful woman, Jess. Beautiful and special. U desrve 2 b satisfied. U desrve 2 have evry desire met.

Mmmm, Jayson.

R u touchng urslf?

Yesss.

Good.

R u?

My hand is arnd my tip rght now.

Your tip is so thick.

Wld u stroke it if I were thre?

O yes.

Wld u tke it in ur mouth?

I would tke all of it.

All of it?

All of it.

I wnt u, Jess. I've wntd u since bfre I even saw ur pic. I jst felt smthng wth u. A connection

I . . . I knw wht u mean.

U do?

Yes. I've tried to deny it, but I can't. As wrong as it is, I think abt u a lot. I long 4 our chats.

Our conversations flow, dn't thy?

Yes, they do.

Is ur hand still on ur pussy?
Yes.
Do u have fngrs insde of it?
I do.
How many?
Two.
Can u get 3?
I can get 4.
Wow!
R u still strokng?
On the vrge of explodng.
Mmm. Shame it has 2 go 2 waste.
Maybe I day it wn't hve 2.
U never knw.

Jayson grinned again. She was wrong. He did know.

He was rock hard. I'm abt 2 cum, Jess.

He stroked his manhood faster, held on to it tighter.

Mmmmmm. I wish I cld see.
If it were ur turn u cld dare me 2 capture tht.
Do we hve 2 take turns?
Truth or dare. We hve 2 follw the rules.
Is all of ths jst a game 2 u, Jayson?
Not at all, Jess.
OK.
So ... truth or dare?
I'll switch it up this time. Truth.

Jayson moved his hand up and down faster. As he did, he imagined Jess stroking him. He imagined being inside of her mouth. She'd chosen truth. He'd known she would, and his knowing made the moment that much more erotic.

His right hand stroking, he typed with his left.

Do u want 2 meet me?

The friction of his skin against his skin was incendiary. He stroked and thought of Jess on him. He already knew what her answer was going to be.

She typed, Yes.

Jayson erupted. He worked his hands as he did, making his eruption flow harder. "Jesssss," he whispered.

Jayson, I don't wnt 2, but I hve 2 go. My daughter jst woke up 2 go 2 the bathroom.

OK.

I'm sorry. We'll continue ths again.

Defntly. But bfre u go, Jess, I hve I qstn.

Yes?

Did u hve an orgsm?

Yes! Did u?

I did.

Wish I cld hve seen.

It's ur turn 2 ask nxt time.

Lookng forward 2 it.

So am I.

OK . . . hve 2 run. Talk 2 u soon.

OK. I'll b thnkng abt u, Jess.

I will 2. Bye.

Jess exited from AOL, and Jayson sat still with his hand around his shaft. *Soon,* he thought. Soon they were going to meet, and when they did, their forever was going to begin. Jayson grabbed his cell phone. He wanted to send Jess another picture to remember him by.

Chapter 13

Jess didn't want to end the conversation, but she had to because of her oldest daughter's sudden appearance in the dining room to announce that she had to go to potty. Jess quickly adjusted the panties she wore. They were now soaked. Her daughter had appeared so quickly and silently, that she'd only had time to remove her fingers from inside of her vagina. Jess quickly sent her daughter on her way, and then reluctantly said good night to Jayson and logged out of AOL.

Now she shook her head. What if her daughter had seen her? What could she have possibly given as a viable explanation for sitting in the chair by the dining table with her head pressed back into the chair, her legs spread wide, and her middle finger moving back and forth inside of what she'd explained to her girls was something no one should ever touch? She'd been so lost in the heat of the sexual encounter Jayson's words and picture had created in her mind that she had forgotten that she wasn't alone.

Jess closed her legs, the tip of her clit still pulsating, as her daughter flushed the toilet from the bathroom a few feet away. Never in her life had she ever done something so morally wrong. She was no prude and had done wild things in her younger days, but she was either single or just "dating." Marriage and motherhood had been nowhere on the horizon.

She was wrong. Absolutely and shamefully wrong. And the worst part was that had her daughter not appeared, her finger would still be inside of her, pretending to be Jayson's dick, doing to her what his words on the screen said they would. She shook her head again. She couldn't remember the last time she'd been so aroused, so wet. *Too long*, she thought. *Too damned long.*

"Mommy?"

Jess turned her head. Her daughter was standing just inside of the dining room, rubbing her half-closed eyes. Jess smiled with a hint of a frown pulling down the corners of her mouth ever so slightly. "Hey, honey." She pushed back away from the table, swiveled her chair, and opened her arms wide. "Come here."

Her daughter ambled over to her slowly and fell into her arms. Jess kissed her on the top of her head.

"Why are you still up?" her daughter asked, her tiny head pressing flat against her chest.

"I was studying," Jess replied, hating herself for lying.

"You're always up late studying."

Jess raised her eyebrows. "Well, I have to take care of you and your sister first, so that's the only time I get to do my schoolwork."

"Do you want us to take care of ourselves so that you don't have to stay up late?"

"No, honey. I like taking care of you guys."

"But you don't sleep a lot. And you always say that sleep is important."

"It is, honey," Jess said, kissing her daughter again. "But when you're a mommy, you don't always get to sleep as much as you'd like to."

Her daughter yawned, and then drawled out an, "OK."

Jess kissed her oldest again. "Time for you to go back to bed," she said. She started to rise from her chair, when her cell phone chimed. Her heart thudded. The chime meant another picture had come through.

"Someone's calling you," her daughter said, turning her head toward her phone.

Jess quickly grabbed her cell, pressed a button to stop the chime, and turned her phone facedown. "It's just a message from Daddy."

Her daughter yawned again. "Daddy is always up late too."

"Yes, he is," Jess said, the volume in her voice dipping.

"You should try to be up late together."

Jess raised her eyebrows again. *Kids*, she thought. *Oftentimes they speak nothing but the absolute truth.* "Come on, honey. Let's get you back to bed."

She rose from her chair, and instead of ushering her daughter to her room, she gathered her in her arms and carried her to her room. After tucking her in, planting another kiss on her forehead, along with her sister's forehead, she went back to the dining room and grabbed her phone.

"Oh my," she whispered softly after clicking on OK to view the picture mail Jayson had sent. His dick, bigger than it had been before, filled her screen.

Jayson had asked her if she wanted to meet him. It was a question that she shouldn't have answered. Or, at the very least, one that she shouldn't have answered honestly. But caught up in the heat and intensity of the moment, answer it honestly is what she'd done.

She licked her lips as her thoughts revisited the back and forth sexual exchanges she and Jayson had just had.

Wrong. Dangerous. Exciting. Three words that rode alongside those thoughts, the last one being the most dominant of the three.

Exciting.

As wrong and dangerous as it was, Jess couldn't deny how satisfyingly exciting it was. She looked at Jayson's dick again, and as she did, her hand slithered back down beneath her panties.

Chapter 14

Rita had to go to the police. She'd been tied up with rope, her ankles and wrists fastened to her bedposts. She'd had duct tape pressed over her mouth to stifle her cries for help and mercy. She'd been backhanded and punched. Her blood had flowed. Tears had fallen from her eyes as she was fucked savagely and repeatedly for nearly six hours.

Raped.

She had to go to the police.

But how could she?

There were pictures and chat and text messages that contradicted the truth. There was a marriage, and more important, a company and reputation to keep from being ruined.

How could she go?

Rita rocked back and forth as she sat hugging her knees against her chest in her Jacuzzi/bathtub filled with now lukewarm water. This was her fifth bath, yet she still felt dirty. The clean bill of health given by her doctor, and seemingly an infinite number of soaps she'd tried since Jayson had been inside of her didn't matter. She was filthy. Soiled with his sweat that had been absorbed into the pores of her skin. Desecrated with his saliva she could still feel and smell on her.

Rita shivered, cried, and cursed herself for being foolish and desperate enough to play Jayson Winston's game.

Truth or dare.

She wanted to go to the police, but Jayson had her truths. He had her dares given. Worst of all, he had the dares she had requested.

I wnt 2 b fckd hard and deep.

U wnt it 2 hurt?

Yes! I wnt u to pound me. Make my pussy sore.

I cld fuck u in the worst way, Rita.

Please do!

Rita shivered and cried harder, her body shaking tears. Her own words rocked her to her core. She needed desperately to tell the police what happened. That she had been physically and sexually assaulted. But her words, her requests, her demands . . .

Rita trembled violently. Everyone would know if she said or did anything. Everyone would know what an unfaithful whore she was.

She moaned, and then let out a shrill scream as she released the hold around her knees, closed her eyes, and slid down below the water that was quickly growing cold. As water filled her lungs and a pain that she could have never imagined riddled through her body, she hypocritically wondered how anyone could take her own life.

Chapter 15

Meet me.

Jess stopped breathing and held her breath as she read Jayson's words.

Meet me.

She exhaled slowly as her heart began to beat heavily. It was something she'd been thinking about ever since she responded to his "truth" question. She did want to meet him. It had been an honest answer. It had also been a very scary one, because the truth was something she couldn't run away from, when running away was the very thing she needed to do.

She was married, and she loved her husband, and despite the growing wedge between them, she was faithful to him. At least she was until she'd sent the first picture to Jayson. Yet even with all that she had done since then, technically, she hadn't broken the vows she'd made.

But staring at Jayson's words . . .

Jess breathed slowly while her heart beat with such force she could hear it echo. She looked again at Jayson's words.

Meet me.

A chill ran through her. *End this now*, her voice of reason whispered. *End this before it's too late.*

She continued to look at Jayson's chat message, his request. *Faithful*, she thought. She had promised that. Just as Esias had promised that he would always love and be there for her. But physically, he'd been distant, and emotionally, the gap was even wider. Was she supposed to suffer the effects from his vacancy? Jayson wanted to meet. So did she. But yet, she still hesitated to respond.

R u still thre?

Log out, her conscience said. *This is your last chance to do the right thing.*

Jess?

Another few seconds of nonmovement went by before Jess finally reacted by sitting forward and typing, I'm here. Sorry. Jst had a phone call.

OK. Was jst worried.

Worried? Why?

Bcuz I said 2 meet me.

No worries. Jst a phone call tht I had 2 tke.

OK. So?

So?

Do u wnt 2 do it? Do u wnt 2 meet?

Jess shook her head. It was an involuntary movement because while her head shook, her fingers typed, How?

I can come 2 NY.

I jst realized I never asked where u live!

I'm in Cali.

California! But aren't u a NY Giants fan? Shouldn't ur favorite team b the Raiders or the 49rs?

Lol. Blue has alwys been my fave color, so I gravitated to the G-Men.

OK. California. Wow. Didn't expect tht.

Wht did u expect?

I don't knw. Jst not California. Tht's far.

By car, yes. By plane . . . jst a cple of hrs.

Do u hve family or friends here in NY?

No. I wld be flyng 2 NY jst 2 see u.

Tht's crazy.

The only thng tht's crazy, Jess, is how badly I wnt 2 see u.

I'm married, Jayson, she typed more for herself than for him. We really shldn't go there.

Hvn't we alrdy with our pics and chats?

Yes . . . but

Do u still hve my pics?

Jess took a side glance at her phone. Yes.

Whch ones?

All of them.

Whn was the lst time u lookd at thm? B honst.

Jess ran her hand through her hair. She wanted to lie, needed to. She typed, A half hour ago.

Why did u look at thm?

Bcuz . . .

Bcuz?

Bcuz . . . they're nice pictures.

Whch 1 is ur fave?

I like all of thm.

Pick 1.

Grrr.

Pick. And keep it real.

Jess ruffled her hair again. I'm tryn 2 b good, Jayson.

Why? Hsn't it felt good being bad?

Yes, but I'm married.

And I've seen ur breasts, whch I thnk r prfct by the way.

Jess smiled.

Whch pic do u like, Jess?

Grrr. Ur so bad, Jayson.

4 u . . . yes . . . very. Now pick.

Aren't u being demanding?

4 smthng I wnt . . . hell, yes!

LOL!

So . . . whch is ur fave?

Jess took a deep breath and released it in one hard, long exhale. As much as she needed to fight it, she couldn't. She typed, The pic of your magic stick.

Do u wnt it, Jess?

I . . . I'm married.

Tht's not wht I askd.

You knw the answer already.

R u afraid 2 tell me?

No.

Thn . . . answr.

Fine. Yes. I do.

Thn meet me.

I can't.

Sure u can. I alrdy said I wld come 2 NY.

We shouldn't do this.

But we're gng 2, rn't we?

Jess let out a long, drawn out sigh. Ths is crazy, she typed again.

Whn do u wnt 2 meet?

Jess thought about it for a moment, and before she could stop herself, she answered.

Next weekend my hsbnd is gng 2 Atlanta 4 a producer's seminar.

O yeh?

Yes.

Can u get a sitter 4 ur grls?

They can probably spend the night with their cousin. God, I can't believe I'm doing ths.

U wnt this, Jess. U need it. U need the release. Tht's why ur doing ths.

It's still wrong.

Look at my pics, Jess.

Jess grabbed her cell, scrolled through the picture mail Jayson had sent, and found her favorite picture.

R u lookng at it?

Jess nibbled down on her bottom lip. Yes.

Thnk abt it being insde of u. Can u imagine tht?

Jess moaned, making sure to keep her voice down to avoid waking her daughters. Yes!

I wld luv 2 b deep, Jess. I wld luv 2 satisfy u the way ur hubby isn't.

Mmm.

Jess felt herself growing wet in between her legs. She looked at Jayson's picture again. Four weeks had gone by since she and Esias had had sex. Work, the kids, her online classes, and Esias's need for studio time just gave them little opportunity for intimacy. There were times when a moment or two did arise for them, and when they did, Esias had tried to capitalize. But in the four week's span, things between Jess and Jayson had heated up, and as bad as it was, Jess found herself yearning more for their online times together, than for her chance to be with her husband.

I'm gng 2 come 2 NY nxt wknd, Jess. Make arrngmnts 4 ur grls to stay wth their cousn, and thn plan 2 be fcked like u wnt 2 b.

Jess licked her lips.

You hve a way wth words, Jayson.

I'm jst spkng the truth.

Mmm.

Lstn . . . I hve 2 get gng unfrtnly. My VB semnr is abt 2 begn.

OK.

Make ur plans. I'll b buyng my plne tix to NY aftr my class tnght.

Jess felt her cheeks grow warm. OK.

Nite, sexy. See u in class tmrrw.

Jess smiled. OK.

She logged out of messenger as Jayson's name disappeared. Slowly she shook her head. *So, so wrong,* she thought.

Her conscience's voice, which had been on mute, rose in volume suddenly. *You're going to regret this. You'll see.*

Jess frowned, and then put her conscience back on mute. Right or wrong, she'd made her decision.

Chapter 16

Rita was dead. Suicide by drowning herself in her bathtub. She'd been found by her husband six hours after he returned home from a business trip.

Jayson sat in front of his laptop reading an online article about Rita's death. He'd first found out about it when he signed in to his Visual Basics class and was greeted by a somber message from the professor informing them all that Rita would no longer be with them. He didn't go into details, but he did explain that she had taken her own life. The class had been cancelled, of course, but people had chosen to remain signed into the class to talk. Some students spoke about their online friendship with Rita; others spoke about their own experiences with losing friends and family to suicide. Jayson participated in the banter with a smile on his face.

After that, he did an online search for local news where Rita lived in Los Angeles and got the rest of the details on her tragic, sad, and untimely demise. Her husband was in shock; her friends struggled to deal with the news, as they had never known her to have had any issues.

Her best friend said, "She had everything in life that she wanted. A successful company, a great husband, wonderful, lifelong friends. Never in a million years did I think anything was wrong. I'm just . . . I'm devastated. I can't believe she's gone."

Jayson shook his head with a smirk. Rita. She had everything, but she still had needs. Freaky needs. Needs that he had fulfilled for her. Jayson chuckled, then minimized his screen and went to his desktop. There he double-clicked one folder with Rita's name. When it opened, everything that tied Rita to him appeared. Transcripts of chat messages—all of the pictures she had ever sent him. Jayson shook his head disapprovingly, and then double-clicked on one of the fifteen photographs he possessed. She was posing in front of a mirror, naked from the waist up. Her cell phone was in her right hand, capturing the image. Her breast was in her left hand. This was one of the first pictures she had ever sent him. Jayson had dared her to do it, to hold her breast for him.

He stared at the picture for a few seconds and admired her cosmetically enhanced D-cups. He'd had a good time fondling, squeezing, and sucking on them when he had fucked her. Whoever her surgeon had been, he'd done one hell of a job.

"Oh, well," Jayson said with a shrug. He let his eyes linger on Rita's small nipple for a moment, and then deleted the image, along with all of the other photographs he had. He then deleted the chat messages and, afterward, her folder. When he was finished clearing the desktop, he emptied his recycling bin. "Sayonara, Rita. It was fun while it lasted."

He laughed. Rita had been so easy to manipulate. The easiest one, in fact, because she was rich, and her money had made her arrogant. She thought her shit didn't stink. But it did. That's what attracted Jayson to her in the first place. He enjoyed working her, enjoyed making her do what he wanted her to. He found pleasure in that with all of the women.

But with Jess the pleasure was different.

He leaned back in his chair and thought about her. Thought about how different her energy was; her spirit. She stirred him in a way that none of the others had. That's why she was going to be the last.

Next weekend.

The beginning of forever.

Jayson moved his arrow along the bottom edge of his screen and double-clicked on a folder with Jess's name. Hers was a library he planned to enhance and keep for a very long time.

Chapter 17

"Did you speak to your academic advisor yet?"

Jess pulled her eyebrows down as she looked at her husband curiously. They were at the dining table, along with their girls. It was one of the rare nights they ate together as a complete family. "No. Why?"

Esias took a bite of the pasta on his plate, then took a sip of juice. "I checked the messages on the phone when I got home. There was one from two days ago. Your academic advisor asking you to call her right away to discuss the possibility of you failing your class." He put his fork down, sat back in his chair, and folded his arms across his chest. "I didn't know things were that bad."

Jess slammed her eyebrows together even more. "What do you mean you didn't know? I've been complaining about how difficult things have been."

"Yes, but I never suspected failure was an option. I wish I would have."

Jess pulled her head back. *"Excuse me?* First of all, if you didn't realize I was in danger of failing, it's only because you weren't paying any attention to me. Second of all . . . what do you mean you wished you would have known?"

"I mean that I would have tried to help you somehow had I known."

Jess shook her head. "You're full of it, Esias. I've been complaining and not once did you ever make an attempt to help me."

"Again, had I known things were that bad—"

"So what? . . . I have to be failing before you decide to lend your wife a hand?"

"I'm not saying that, Jess."

Jess slammed her hand down on the tabletop, causing her girls, who'd grown silent and had been watching them with curious eyes, to jump. "So then what the hell exactly are you saying, Esias?"

Esias looked over at the girls, then back at Jess. "Will you calm down," he said, lowering the volume in his voice, trying to take the edge out of it. "I'm not trying to argue."

Unable to rein herself in and follow his lead, Jess said, *"You're not?* Are you *sure* about that? Because I don't see how you're trying to avoid arguing by coming at me the way you did."

Esias exhaled, then looked at their daughters again. "Girls, go to your rooms. Mommy and I need to talk."

"But I'm not finished yet," their oldest protested.

"Me neither," followed her sibling.

"Just take your plates with you and be very careful about making a mess, OK?" Esias instructed.

Both girls looked at each other, and then looked at Jess, who always told them that eating in their rooms was forbidden.

She nodded and said, "Go now, girls."

"Can we turn the TV on?" their youngest asked.

"Sure," Esias said, leaning over and planting a kiss on her forehead. "Just remember . . . no making a mess."

"OK, Daddy."

Both daughters got up from the table, grabbed their plates and minicups, and left the dining room.

When they could be heard in their bedroom upstairs, Esias looked at Jess with a frown. "You're really being ridiculous, Jess. All I was trying to say was that I wish you would have explained better how bad things were. Failing's not something you want to do."

"Oh, well, thank you for helping to clear that up for me, Jayson, because I certainly have been trying my hardest to do that!"

Jess pursed her lips and turned her gaze away from Esias as he stared at her with a hard, unflinching glare. She didn't want or need this. She'd been beating herself up enough as it was for her inevitable failure in her PHP class. A failure that had everything to do with Jayson and the focus that she had placed on chatting and doing things she shouldn't have been doing with him. She had skipped online tutoring sessions. She had been in the weekly seminars, but instead of paying attention to the professor and participating in the discussions, she chatted with Jayson. The fact of the matter was, her outburst to Esias had more to do with her anger and disappointment in herself for ignoring her voice of reason, than it did with the things he had said.

She could feel Esias's gaze on her. She turned her head and looked at him. "What, Esias? What more *advice* do you have to give me?"

Esias narrowed his eyes. "Who's Jayson?" he asked.

Jess's heart dropped into the pit of her stomach. "What?"

"You called me Jayson," Esias said. "Who is that?"

Though not yet visible, Jess could feel her body tremble. She'd said Jayson's name. When?

"Who is he, Jess?" Esias asked again, the edge in his tone sharper.

Jess took a short, quick breath as the temperature beneath her skin rose. She'd said Jayson's name out loud, and not just in her thoughts, which is what she had been doing with him in her mind.

"Who the hell is Jayson?" Esias demanded again, his volume level rising.

Jess swallowed hard. Her hands were flat on the table and while a few seconds ago, her trembling may not have been visible, she knew that were she to lift them, Esias would see them shaking violently.

Esias watched her as he waited for her reply, his eyes dark, his body taut, looking as though he were about to explode.

Jess needed to answer him, and she needed to answer him quickly. She swallowed again. "Jayson," she said, her throat tight, "he's my tutor."

"And why the hell did you call me by your tutor's name?"

Jess shook her head. "Don't take that tone with me, Esias."

Esias pounded his fist down on the table. "You just called me by another man's name, Jess! What do you mean 'don't take that tone'?"

"Jayson is my tutor, Esias. I've been online with him, harassing him, doing all I could to try to pass this god-damned class. I called you by his name only because of this stupid argument we're having! Again . . . it was an accident!"

Esias looked at her, his stare filled with skepticism.

Jess's heart continued to pound as she hoped her words and reactions were believable enough.

"Jayson," Esias said. "You've never mentioned him before."

"He's just my tutor."

"How often do you talk to him?"

Jess looked up at the ceiling. "Oh, Jesus, Esias. I talk to Jayson for help. And like I said, maybe if you had bothered to care about my classes, you would have heard me mention him."

"That's bullshit, Jess. I've asked how things were going before. Hell, I asked you last week how things were, and you chewed my head off, remember?"

Jess groaned and ran her hands furiously through her hair. "I've been stressed, Esias. Talking about school has been the last thing I wanted to do, OK? Shit!"

Esias watched her as she shoved both hands through her hair again. "So," he said after a few long seconds of silence, "this Jayson. Do you deal with him a lot when I'm not here?"

Jess threw her hands in the air. "Christ! He's my tutor!"

"It was just a fucking question, Jess."

"No . . . it's an accusation, and it's bullshit. I have enough on my mind. I don't need this." Jess pushed her chair back hard from the table and stood up.

"I didn't accuse you of anything," Esias countered.

Jess curled her lips. "Whatever, Esias. Whatever you say."

As quickly as she could, she stormed away from the table. As she did, her voice of reason skipped behind her and whispered, *I told you so.*

Chapter 18

I hve my ticket.

U do?

Yeh. I fly in @ 4 in the afternoon on Fri.

Wow!

Wht?

UR really coming.

I said I was. Did u thnk I wsn't serious?

No.

Bcuz I'm very serious, Jess. U said u wntd 2 see me. That u wntd 2 b wth me. That u wntd me 2 help ease ur stress. Were u jst tlkng shit or did u mean evrythng u said?

I'm serious, Jayson. As wrng as this is . . . I'm serious. I wnt 2 see u.

R u gng to b shy whn we're face 2 face?

I . . . I don't knw. I've never done anything like this bfre.

Can I ask u a qstn?

Of course.

U said as wrng as ths is . . . do u thnk ths is wrng?

I'm married.

I rmembr u mentioning smthng abt a hsbnd.

Funny. Seriously . . . I'm married and I'm a mother.

A MILF!

I'm tryn 2 explain why ths is wrng. Stop distracting me!

LOL! OK. Contnue on wth tryn 2 expln how smthng so obvsly rght cld possibly b wrng.

Sigh. I promised God 2 honor and respect my marriage. I vowed 2 b faithful.

Jess . . . didn't ur hsbnd promise 2 care 4 u?

Yes.

And didn't he promise 2 put nothng and no one abve u?

Yes, but . . . it's not tht simple.

Wht cld be simpler thn luvng and pleasing u, Jess? I mean really, tht's all he has 2 do. Luv u, tke care of u, pay attn 2 u. Make sure tht there's nvr a doubt in ur mind how spcl u r 2 him. How beautiful u r 2 him. Tht's all he has 2 do. Rght?

Yes.

So thn why isn't he doing it? Why isn't he home gvng u the attn u deserve? Why isn't he thre now makng luv 2 u?

He . . . he's busy.

Tht's no excuse, Jess, and u knw it. I bet no mattr how busy ur life became, u always made time 4 him.

Yes. I did.

I bet he nevr had 2 deal wth u not pyng attn 2 his needs.

No. He didn't.

So thn wht's really wrng, Jess? The fact tht ur husbnd neglcts u emotionally and physically, or the fact tht since we've knwn one anthr, u've nvr felt more stimulated? I hvn't been inside of u yet, Jess, yet I'm stsfyng u in a way ur hsbnd hsn't and can't. Isn't tht rght?

Yes.

So how is tht wrng?

I . . . I

Ur married but ur hsbnd's not. Not the way u desrve, Jess. Unless u back out and stnd me up, I'm gng 2 shw u ths wknd wht u desrve. That is a promise tht I'll fulfill multiple times.

Multiple?

If u can hndle it.

If u can give it u mean.

O trust me, gorgeous, I can.

If my grls ever did anything like ths I'd strangle thm.

Well, let's hope ur grls find the rght man 2 b wth.

Hmm.

Dammit I can't wait 4 Fri.

I'm excited 2!

I'm gng 2 make sure u explde, Jess. I'm gng 2 make sure ur body purrs 4 me.

Mmmm. Tht sounds good.

Don't hld bck, OK. I wnt u 2 let it all go. My dick is urs to dominate. OK?

Mmm. OK!

U promise?

I do.

I'm hldng u 2 tht.

U can.

Good. Unfrtnly I hve some errands 2 run.

OK. O wait . . . bfre u go. Where r u gng 2 b staying when u come 2 town?

I hve a room bookd at the Gramercy Park Hotl in Midtown.

The Gramercy. Expensive!

I'm gng 2 fulfill u, sexy. I wnted ur nght wth me 2 b smthng u wldn't forgt.

Sounds so good.

Ur gng 2 b my prisoner, Jess. R u ready 4 tht?

Defntly.

Good. Thn on Fri @ 6, I'll expct to get a call frm u sayng that u r in the lobby downstairs.

OK!

Untl Fri.
Untl Friday.

Jayson signed out of AOL, shut his laptop, and set it down beside him on the passenger seat of his Escalade. He smiled and took a breath in through his nostrils. He could still smell Debra from his Networking Administration class. He had fucked her so good in his backseat right in front of her home. She'd done so much talking about it being crazy of them to be out in front that way, yet when she set foot inside of his leather-clad interior, all apprehension she had, had disappeared. Debra had been loud when she'd ridden him, and she'd been even louder when he took her from behind.

Jayson took another whiff of sex scented with berries. Debra. Maybe after New York, he'd make a trip back to Houston for one final fuck. Perhaps he'd leave her pregnant too, the way he had Alisa.

He chuckled to himself as he thought of Alisa's chat message to him saying that she was pregnant. He would have loved to have seen the look on her face when she discovered she was. That shouldn't have happened because they had been safe and had used condoms. But Alisa didn't know that he'd stuck a needle through the condom he had used.

Jayson chuckled again.

Women were such beautiful whores. Famous words spoken by his father, who had shown him at an early age how easy it was to manipulate them.

"Women are toys," he'd said. "You play with them, and then get rid of them before they get too worn. A worn-out toy is never fun to play with."

"But what about Mommy? How come you haven't gotten rid of her yet?"

"You always keep one special toy for display, li'l man. Remember that. In a sea of whores, there's one female out there that's a cut above the rest. No matter what you do, you make sure you find that special one. The rest you just fuck and throw away."

Jayson nodded his head as he turned it and looked out through the tint of his driver's window and watched Jess's husband emerge from his job.

During one of their conversations, Jess had mentioned the printing company Esias worked for. After a quick online search, Jayson had the address to the sole New York location. The next day he flew to the city to see him.

With an elongated box filled with six roses, Jayson walked into the building Esias worked in, approached an overweight security guard sitting behind a counter almost too small for his hefty frame, and announced that he had a delivery for Esias Richards. Minutes later, after a quick call from the guard, Esias appeared from an elevator off to the right.

Jayson had clenched his jaw tightly as Esias approached and stared at him with a scrutinizing eye. He was taller than he'd expected, about five feet ten, five feet eleven, with a slightly athletic frame and a small paunch in his midsection. His hair was shaved low all the way around. He had a goatee connected to a thin line of hair that outlined his jawline and connected to his sideburns. *Not bad looking,* Jayson thought, *but definitely not a complement to Jess's beauty.* Not the way he knew he was.

"Those are for me?" Esias asked, coming to a stop in front of him.

Jayson, wearing khaki shorts, a white T-shirt, with white sneakers on his feet, a pair of shades, and a New York Yankees visor around his head, nodded and said, "Are you Esias Richards?"

"I am."

Jayson held out the box. "Then these are yours."

Esias looked at him with a skeptical eye. "Who are they from?"

Jayson stared at Esias for a brief second that to him felt like hours and imagined shoving the bone of his nostril up into his brain before replying, "Dude, I don't know. I just deliver the stuff."

By the look in his eyes, Esias hadn't been happy with Jayson's response. Unflinching, Jayson stared back, his heart pounding, his body tense. He thought again about hitting Esias viciously, but the guard was there watching. Besides, that would have ruined everything, so he forced his expression to soften and said, "Are you going to take them, or should I just throw them out?"

Esias looked at him for another moment, and then shrugged. "I'll take it."

Jayson handed him the box.

"Is there anything I need to sign?"

Jayson shook his head. "Nope," and then turned to leave.

As he did, the guard said to Esias, "They from your wife?"

Jayson began to walk away slowly, and as he did, he heard Esias open the box. Inside, Jayson had placed a small card that read: *Truth or dare?*

Nearing the entrance door, he heard Esias say, "It's from my wife. She says she loves me."

"Nice," the guard replied.

Jayson walked out of the building with a smile, knowing the roses would only end up in the garbage. He was determined more than ever to make Jess his.

Jess.

So special, Jayson thought. She was the one he was supposed to have. The special one among the sea of whores.

He watched as Esias made his way to a Camry half-way down the block. "Your time is up," he said. "You've had her long enough."

He thought momentarily about following Esias home, but as badly as he wanted to see his woman, he didn't want to push it, so he started his Escalade, put it in drive, and pulled into traffic and headed in the opposite direction to go back to the Gramercy Hotel.

Three days, he thought. He would need a fuck before then to occupy his time.

Chapter 19

"Thank you so much, Courtney, for letting the girls stay over."

Jess's sister smiled. "No problem, sis. I don't get to see my nieces enough anyway."

"That's because you're always on the road."

Courtney shrugged. "The life of a sister trying to make it."

Jess smiled. She'd been listening to her sister's demo CD on the way over. "I think this is going to be the one, girl. I listen to it all the time."

Grinning proudly, Courtney said, "Esias gave me some great material. Just wait until you hear it when everything is mixed properly."

"I can't wait."

Courtney turned her head as a loud bang erupted in her apartment behind her. She opened her apartment door. "Ladies!" she said forcefully. "If you break it, you buy it back!" She turned and winked at Jess.

Jess called out to her girls, who both appeared at the door's threshold. "I don't need to remind you two to behave, do I?" Jess asked.

"No, Mommy!" both girls answered in unison.

"Good answer. Now . . . I'll be back to get you tomorrow afternoon, OK?"

"OK!"

Both girls were fidgety, itching to get back to the romping they'd been doing with their two cousins. Jess leaned forward, planted kisses on both of their cheeks, and as she did, a feeling of guilt came over her. She was getting rid of them to go and be with a man that wasn't their father. The guilt that encompassed her wasn't because of that fact, but rather because she couldn't seem to get going fast enough.

She hugged her daughters, and then let them run off. She then stood up, looked at her sister, and said, "Thanks again. I owe you big time. With Esias going away, I really need the night to focus on my schoolwork."

"Like I said, girl, it's not a problem."

Jess gave her a hug. "Love you."

"I love you back," Courtney replied.

Jess waved good-bye and headed to her car. All that was left now was to drive Esias to the airport; and then she would do what she knew she shouldn't do.

Chapter 20

Six weeks ago . . .

Reggie . . . before you read what I have to say, please know that despite what it's going to seem like, I did love you with all my heart. You treated me like no man ever had before. With respect, with kindness. You were selfless with your love, Reggie. No matter the time or day, you loved me unconditionally. There was never a day that went by when I didn't look at you and know that, in you, I had a man that loved me and not the money I had. You were a godsend. A knight in shining armor, and I wish I had been as self-giving, as honorable, as you were. But I wasn't.

I was unfaithful to you and your love, and just writing these words makes the pain for my foolishness hurt even more. I did things, Reggie, things I'm so ashamed of. Please believe me, Reggie, I wasn't unfaithful to you because I was unhappy, because that wasn't the case. In fact, I was very happy. You may find it hard to believe after you read about all of the things I've done, but I swear to you that I was so very, very happy. I was also selfish. And my selfishness caused me to do things that no wife should ever do. It also caused me to be raped, and ultimately, it caused my death.

Reggie Starks looked away from the handwritten letter he'd found in the inside pocket of his black suit and let out a hard, grief-stricken breath of air as the ground which had already been crumbling to pieces now fell apart completely.

His wife had been unfaithful.

She had been raped.

And now he was gripping tightly, with violently trembling hands, her suicide note.

Tears rained down from Reggie's eyes. He hadn't known what to think when he discovered the letter in his pocket. It was the day of his wife's funeral. He had just gotten dressed. He was numb when he did. He had been ever since he walked in and discovered Rita's lifeless body submerged in their large bathtub.

Initially he thought she was playing around with him, so he put his hand over her forehead to hold her down, expecting her to sit up right away with a gasp. She didn't have a fear of water, but what she did have a fear of was being held down. Reggie had had a smile on his face with his hand on her forehead, but that smile had quickly disappeared when his wife didn't jump up.

Panic had taken hold of his throat and squeezed his windpipe so hard that he couldn't breathe as she lay still under the water with vacant, terrified eyes staring into nothing. Shock kept him rooted to the marble flooring of the bathroom. Disbelief kept his mouth opened wide, with no sound being released.

He'd stood rigid, frozen in fear as seconds ticked by with the urgency of a snail making its way one inch to the next. Eventually, he found the will to make himself move to the tub to gather his wife into his arms. He called her name over and over until he realized that no matter how many times he called, or how much he shook, pleaded, and caressed her, she wasn't going to respond.

She was dead. And try as he had to not accept it, he'd known she was dead the second he'd put his hand against her skin, which had been much colder than the water she lay in.

Reggie cried as his body shook. He gripped his wife's letter so tightly, the edges were crinkling. He didn't want to read on, but he had to. There was more that his wife had to say. Somehow, he lifted the 8 x 11 piece of paper to an angle below his eyes and continued.

I was chatting online with Jayson Winston from my Visual Basics class. It was innocent at first, but the topics of our chats quickly crossed lines and became filthy discussions about sex. That's when the game of truth and, primarily, dare, began.

Jayson dared me to do things that, God, I regret so much now. I . . . I sent pictures to him. Pictures of the most private parts of my body. I sent pictures of myself doing things to those private parts. Reggie, I . . . I thought what I was doing was just harmless fun. I didn't think things would escalate, but they did. The truths became truer, the dares became bolder. I hate to admit it, but I started to become hooked on the freakiness. I started to not only look forward to being bad, but needing to be as well, and as my needs intensified, my desire to make the words and actions in the picture become reality grew stronger, to the point where I just had to make them come true.

And that's when I made the terrible decision to physically cheat on you.

It . . . it was a dare. We were supposed to have sex. We were supposed to do things . . . well, he was supposed to do things to me. Nasty things. I . . . I wanted to be tied up. I wanted to be gagged. And . . . and I wanted to be fucked. It was a fantasy of mine that he promised to fulfill. But instead of doing that, he raped me, Reggie. He wrapped ropes around my ankles and wrists and tied me to the bedposts. He covered my mouth with duct tape. He hit me and told me to keep quiet; and then he violated me viciously for hours. I screamed, Reggie. I screamed so loud, but no one could hear me. I tried to beg him to stop. I offered him money. A lot of money. But . . . but he didn't want any.

I . . . I wanted to tell you, Reggie. I wanted to tell the police what had happened, but I couldn't because Jayson had everything. Every picture. Every sex-filled discussion. He . . . he threatened to expose what I'd done and tell everyone—friends, family, employees, the media, you. I couldn't . . . couldn't let him do that, so I kept quiet and tried to deal with everything. But the guilt . . . Day after day, it tore me apart. Day after day, I died more and more, and I began to go crazy. Killing myself, oh, God, I can't believe I'm writing this, but killing myself was the only way for me to escape from the hell of what I'd done. It was also the only way to get Jayson back for what he did to me without having my reputation and company ruined.

I realize that's selfish of me, but in this final and absolute moment, I'm just going to be honest. I didn't want my name to be dragged through the mud. I didn't want my friends and family and company to be rocked by a scandal. This was the only way to keep that from happening. I'd rather people talk and speculate about suicide, than have actual proof of my transgressions.

Please forgive me, Reggie. I know I have no right to ask you to, but I am asking. Please. I also have one more thing to ask . . .

I don't think I'm the only person Jayson has done this to. I think—no, I'm sure—there are others. He has to be stopped, Reggie. He's ruining lives.

During one of our chats, Jayson told me about a new class he was going to start taking. A Java Scripts class. Reggie . . . I want you to register for the class as a female. I have a feeling that Jayson will reach out to you. If he does, I want you to respond to him, begin chatting and playing his truth or dare game that I know he will want to play. When the game begins, I want you to escalate it and get him to meet you. I won't tell you what to do when/if you do meet him, but I will say again, that he has to be stopped for good.

Reggie . . . I'm so sorry for what I've done. I pray to God that I get to meet you in another lifetime. If I do get that opportunity, I swear to you that I won't waste it. I love you, Reggie. Good-bye.

Still clutching Rita's letter in one hand, Reggie's arms dropped to his sides. He slumped down in the chair he was sitting in and dropped his chin to chest as all the air in his body sighed away. The words on the paper seemed surreal and almost impossible to believe. Yet, his wife was dead.

Dead.

Reggie cried, shook, crumpled up his wife's note in his hand, and then threw it across the room with a growl. He shook his head, wanting so badly for his reality to be a horrible dream.

"Rita," he whispered. There was a knot so thick in his throat that barely a sound escaped. "Rita."

He was burying her in a few hours. That's why he had his black suit on. He'd been to several funerals in the past year, and he always wore this particular suit. Rita had joked once and called it his mortician's suit. Reggie shivered as he imagined her sliding the letter into his inside pocket.

"Rita," he whispered again.

He raised his head and looked over at the bed. His wife had been there sprawled, tied, gagged just weeks ago. He looked across the room and settled his eyes on the crumpled letter. His wife's last words. She'd lied, she'd cheated, while he loved her with all his heart. He should hate her for that. He should be happy that she was gone. But how could he be when he still loved her with every fiber of his being?

Reggie stared at the letter and thought about Rita's request. *Jayson Winston.* She was sure she wasn't the only one, and one thing Reggie knew about his wife was that she was never wrong when she was sure.

Jayson Winston. He'd be joining a Java Scripts class.

Reggie stood up, walked over to the letter, bent down, and picked it up. Rita wanted him to get Jayson to meet him. She hadn't said what she wanted him to do if the opportunity came, but Reggie knew what he would do.

He reached into his pocket, removed a cigarette lighter, and went into the bathroom. He stared at himself in the mirror, looked at his eyes, and saw someone he didn't recognize. Then he flicked the lighter, bringing flame to light, and set it beneath his wife's letter. As it caught on fire, he dropped it into the sink, and as Rita's words disappeared, he thought about registering for class before the burial.

Chapter 21

"Do you have plans tonight?"

Jess's heart thumped. "Excuse me?" She had just pulled to a stop beside the curb in front of the drop-off for passengers flying on Southwest Airlines. She turned her head and faced her husband. "What do you mean do I have plans?"

Esias cocked an eyebrow. "I mean for you and the girls. Do you have anything planned?"

Jess's heart hammered beneath her chest. *Calm down*, she thought. *He doesn't know anything.* She took a breath and let it out slowly. "Oh . . . no. Not really. Maybe we'll get a movie on-demand or something. Why?"

"I just figured you might do something special with me being gone this weekend."

Jess shook her head. "No . . . nothing."

"Maybe you should. It's not often you get a 'girls only' weekend."

Jess shrugged. "We'll see. I still have finals coming, so it's not like I don't have work to do."

Esias raised his eyebrows up and down. "You going to be talking to Jayson this weekend?"

Jess rolled her eyes. Ever since her slipup a little over a week ago, Esias had made it a point to find a way to bring up Jayson's name. "Maybe, Esias. It depends on how stuck I get. Is that all right with you?"

"Relax with the attitude, Jess. It was just a question."

"I'm not the one with the attitude," she replied.

"All I did was ask a question."

"One that was really necessary to ask, right?"

Esias tapped his index finger on his passenger-door panel. "It was a valid question."

"Oh, come off of it, Esias. Ever since I *accidentally* said his name, you've found a way to come up with *valid* questions or statements with his name attached. It's getting old."

Esias worked his jaw. "You called me by his name, Jess."

"We were arguing about school. He's my online tutor. How many times do I have to say that it was unintentional?"

"I understand that we were having a *discussion*, Jess, but the fact remains you called me by his name. Whether you want to admit it or not, as far as I'm concerned, *he* must have been on your mind."

Jess sucked her teeth. "Oh, please—"

"Please what, Jess? I'm not calling you by another woman's name, no matter how much she may have to do with whatever it is we'd be talking about."

"Well, forgive me for not being perfect like you are," Jess said, rolling her eyes.

"I'm not saying I'm perfect, Jess. I'm just saying that was one hell of a mistake to make."

"Again . . . imperfection is a flaw of mine."

"Have you ever spoken to him aside from tutoring?"

Jess placed her elbows against the steering wheel and put her hand over her forehead. Esias's comments and questions were the last thing she needed right now. "Unbelievable," she said. "I can't believe you just asked me that."

"It's not a far-fetched question."

"It's a ridiculous question. And one I'm not going to answer."

"Why not? Do you have something to hide?"

Jess shook her head. Guilt had been weighing down on her ever since she had dropped the girls off at her sister's apartment, and more than once, she had actually considered not going through with the very wrong plans she'd made. But the more Esias hit the nail on the head, the angrier she became and the more she wanted to do what she shouldn't. The more she wanted the release. The more she yearned for the fulfillment of the words she and Jayson had exchanged. She took a slow breath in and on exhale said, "Don't you have a flight to catch?"

"You never answered my question," Esias said, his voice low.

Jess sighed. "And I'm not going to."

Esias sucked in his top lip and gnawed on it with his bottom teeth. "It's an easy question to answer."

Jess let out a frustrated breath. "I'm holding up other cars," she said.

Esias shook his head. "Unbelievable."

"Yes, this is."

Esias opened his car door, stepped out, slammed it shut, and then opened the passenger door, grabbed his carry-on bag from the backseat, and then slammed that door shut too. Without a good-bye, he walked away.

Jess released a breath that she had been holding. She'd held it with the expectation of releasing it with a tirade with his next comment or question. She was thankful that hadn't happened because she knew there was a very good chance she was going to say things she would regret. She watched Esias walk into the airport terminal, and then put her blinkers on and pulled away from the curb.

***

An hour later, she was dressed wearing a pair of dark blue jeans and a white silk blouse that slouched at the neckline. Open-toed pumps were on her feet. She wanted to be sexy, but not overdone. The jeans hugged her ass enough to make a man want to grab hold, and the blouse fight tightly enough up top to accentuate her breasts, but was loose enough to conceal her slight belly. It had taken her forty-five minutes to settle on the outfit. In an overnight bag, she had another pair of jeans and top, and lingerie—just in case.

She looked at herself in the mirror of her dressing table. Mascara had been applied; blush blended in; dark red lipstick was on. She never needed much more than that. "Are you sure?" she asked herself.

Her reflection stared back at her with steady eyes as it gave her a single nod.

"OK."

She raised her hand. In it was her cell phone. She found Jayson's number and sent him a text letting him know that she was on the way. A minute later, Jayson responded with a smiley face.

Jess took one final glance in the mirror, gave her reflection a nod back, and then walked out of the bedroom with dirty thoughts on her mind.

Chapter 22

She was on her way. Finally their moment, their magic was going to happen. Their beautiful music was going to be created.

Jayson couldn't wait.

His father would have been proud of him. If only he were around to see the special woman he'd chosen. But lung cancer had done him in before his time. The doctor had warned him about smoking, but his father never listened. He lived by his own rules.

"Do what you want to do," he often instructed Jayson. "Don't let anybody tell you what you can and can't do. Don't let anybody say what you can and can't have."

Jayson had the utmost respect for his father. He was a man's man. Tall, muscular, strong, proud. His father was the master of his domain, and Jayson admired that. He had tried to find that special female before his father had passed, but his father's health had taken a turn for the worse far sooner than had been expected.

Losing his father had a profound effect on him and made him much more determined to find that special one. Special like his mother, who he still loved with all his heart, even though she had married another man less than six months after his father passed away and had very little contact with him since. Jayson didn't take her lack of communication personally. She was grieving over the loss of a great man. And because Jayson looked just like him, it was tough for his mother to see him.

Jayson understood.

He looked down at his laptop. Regina had sent him another chat message. She was in the new Java Scripts class he'd started.

Jayson . . . r u still thre?

Jayson smiled. Regina was a freak who loved the camera. He typed, I am. I had a call I had 2 tke.

O, OK. I thght maybe my dare was 2 much.

No . . . not at all. But r u sure tht's wht u wnt?

Yes! I wnt u 2 fck me. I wnt u 2 do all of the things my husband won't do. I'm getting wet now jst thnkng abt it. I wish u were here fckng me rght now.

If I cld b, I wld, Regina. Hell . . . I will.

Whn? I need u inside of me.

U tell me. My schedule is opn.

What abt next Saturday? My husband has 2 go away. I'll b free.

Free and clear 2 b fcked?

2 b pounded. I want u 2 do any and everything u wnt 2 do.

I'm gtng hrd imagning all of the thngs I'm gng 2 do 2 u, Regina.

God, I can't wait.

So . . . nxt Sat?

Yes!! He'll b gone.

OK.

R u sure u r gng 2 fulfill ur dare?

I'll surpass it, Regina. I hpe ur pussy will be rdy.

O it will b.

Good! Listn, I hve 2 go. I hve smthng I need 2 do.

OK. Will u b back on later?

I dn't knw. Gng to b prtty busy. I'll try if I can.

OK. I'll keep checking jst in case.

OK.

Jayson signed out of the messenger and laughed. His father had been so right. Women were whores. Except for the special ones.

He shut down his laptop. He wouldn't be on it for at least two days. Or so he hoped. He went into the bathroom to get ready for Jess's arrival.

Chapter 23

Reggie Starks wanted to grab his laptop and throw it against the wall. He hated this, hated what he had to do. But he had to in order to get revenge, retribution. He had to endure the filthy conversations. He had to continue paying money to the prostitute that he had living in the spare bedroom temporarily so that he would have access to photographs when they were requested, which had been often because Jayson loved his pictures.

The hooker's cooperation and silence didn't come cheap, but he didn't care. As disgusting as he felt, he would continue with his mission until he got the end result he needed. Jayson had to pay for what he'd done. Reggie just had to endure.

Next Saturday.

He closed his eyes tightly, trying to keep the well of tears that had risen from spilling over, but grief, shock, disbelief, and rage made the flood impossible to contain.

Next Saturday.

Jayson Winston was going to get his.

Chapter 24

Jess could barely breathe as her heart beat in triplets beneath her chest. She was standing in the lobby of the Gramercy Hotel. Her legs felt like rubber; her hands were cold, clammy, while the rest of her body was warm. Nervous, excited, and apprehensive all combined to set her nerves on fire.

She stood rooted on the red carpeting with the letters G.P.H. in white stitched in its center, and marveled at the splendor around her. Lavish, red furniture; a massive fireplace; a three-tier crystal chandelier; and colorful, expressive paintings adorned the walls. Jess had known of the Gramercy and how lush it was, but, because of the cost, never did she think she would set foot inside. Had her nervous excitement not already done it, the sight of what she was surrounded by would have surely taken her breath away.

She moved slowly along the carpet and made her way down the lobby to the lounge. People were inside, sitting on plush beige and light red-colored chairs and love seats around small round tables with candles placed in the middle. Some sat at the bar, sipping mixed drinks and beers, engaged in conversations. As she made her way to an empty chair, she couldn't help but feel as though any second, one, or all of them, was going to turn around and level scrutinizing eyes on her that questioned just what she was doing there. But, as she sat down, the conversations around her continued without a pause or a dip in volume. She crossed her legs, took a short breath, and let it out slowly in an attempt to ease the excited tension, and then pulled her cell out of her small purse and typed a simple message to Jayson. I'm here.

A minute later, Jayson responded. Coming now!

The pace of Jess's heartbeat quickened. He was coming. There was no turning back now.

Or was there?

Her voice of reason began to yell, began to plead for her to get up before it was too late.

Instead, she took in a breath, looked at the people around her, and wondered how many of them had just sent text messages announcing their arrival.

Her conscience screamed!

Jess exhaled, tightened her hand around her purse, uncrossed her legs, and prepared to stand, prepared to finally listen, to run away.

"Jess?"

Jess paused. Both feet were down, one flat, the other on its toes, preparing to propel her to an upright position. The voice she'd never heard—she'd wanted to, but had never made that dare—but she knew to whom it belonged. Her heart pounded. Everything seemed to slow down; people around her disappeared. A chill ran through her.

She looked up slowly. Standing a few feet in front of her was the man from the pictures. The man with the deep-set eyes, the full lips, the muscular jaw, the well-defined shoulders, the sculpted chest, the penis with girth—*that* man stood before her, looking all too sexy in a pair of dark blue jeans, a form-fitting baby-blue T-shirt with a stylish, black blazer on. "Jayson," she said in a whisper.

She smiled.

Jayson smiled back. "You're here."

Jess gave a nod. "I'm here."

Jayson held out his hand. Jess took it and was surprised by how cold it was. *Cold hands, warm heart*, she thought. She stood up.

"You look amazing," Jayson said. "In pictures you're stunning, but in person . . . you're without equal."

Jess felt her cheeks redden. She was glad she'd taken on her father's darker shade. "Thank you," she said. "You look very handsome as well."

Jayson flashed a sly smile and said quietly, "You're lucky there are people around."

Jess chuckled. "So . . . does that mean I'll be unlucky later on?"

"Very unlucky, Jess. *Very*."

She laughed.

So did Jayson, before he unexpectedly enveloped her in his arms. "I'm sorry," he said, holding her firmly. "But I couldn't fight it anymore. I needed to hold you."

Jess flattened her head against his chest and listened to his heartbeat. "Don't apologize. I wanted to be held. You smell good. I love a man that smells good."

"In that case, let me go upstairs and take a quick bath in my cologne."

Jess laughed. "Overkill is a turnoff."

"I'll stay just the way I am then."

"Wise decision."

Jayson tightened his hold on her.

Jess welcomed it and pressed her body into his even more.

They stood firmly against each other, unmoving, unspeaking for several seconds before Jayson said, "Jess?"

"Yes, Jayson?"

"I know there are people around, but can I kiss you?"

Jess took in a slow breath of air. *This is so wrong,* she thought. *I have no right being there.* On exhale, she said, "Please do."

Jayson took his hand, put it beneath her chin, and tilted her head upward as he angled his down. For the briefest of moments, he looked into her eyes, and when he did, Jess saw a desire, a need in them that she hadn't seen in a man's eyes in a very long time.

"You're beautiful, Jess," he said. And then he pressed his lips against hers.

Jess felt the ground move beneath her feet as her body swooned. Eagerly, she parted her lips to receive his tongue, which had been asking to be let inside. Like familiar lovers on the dance floor, their tongues moved to a sensuous rhythm.

Wrong, Jess thought as she became lost in the kiss. *Wrong, but so deliciously right.*

A few more passionate seconds passed before Jayson pulled himself away and let out a whoosh of air. "OK . . . before I really say to hell with the people around, I better stop."

Jess wiped her lips with her fingers and smiled.

"You're an amazing kisser," he said.

"Thank you. You use your lips well too." *Just like I knew you would.*

"How your husband lets your lips go to waste I don't understand."

Jess shrugged, but didn't say anything, hoping that would be the last time Esias was brought up.

"So . . . are you hungry?"

Jess gave a nod. Nerves had kept her from eating much throughout the day. "I am."

"Do you like Italian?"

"I do."

"The restaurant here, Maialino, has great Italian cuisine."

"Sounds perfect."

Jayson smiled, leaned forward, kissed her deeply again, and then pulled back, grabbed hold of her hand, and led the way.

Chapter 25

"Wait! We . . . I . . . I can't. We need to stop."

Jess flattened her palms against Jayson's chest. They were in his hotel suite. Naked on the bed. Their bodies covered with a light sheen of perspiration—the result of the partial fulfillment of the truth or dare they had been playing.

I dare u 2 let me devour u whn I see u, Jess. I dare u 2 lay back and let go.

Let go.

After Mojitos, chicken penne, and easy, flirtatious conversation at Maialino's. After the ride in the elevator up to Jayson's floor, a ride dominated by groping, kissing, moaning, growling. After bursting into Jayson's room and removing their clothing frantically as though they had a timer to beat and doing it before the timer buzzed would win them the million-dollar prize. After throwing pillows to the floor and tossing the spread and sheet aside—

Jess had let go and let Jayson.

Let him kiss the nape of her neck. Let him trail his way down to her breasts. Let him circle her erect nipples with his tongue. Let him suck and nibble on them. Let him take as much of them in his mouth as he could.

Breathing heavily with eyes closed, Jess let Jayson run his hands down her sides, to her legs. She let him follow behind his hands with his tongue and lips, licking and kissing. And when his hands eased her legs apart, his fingers worked their way up the inside of her thighs and slid into her incredibly moist vagina where they did two steps and pirouettes before his tongue followed after to pop-lock, rumba, and fox trot deeply between her walls, Jess continued to let go. She took the oral pleasure Esias wouldn't give, the pleasure that had her biting down on her lip, moaning loudly. She took it all selfishly. And after she erupted with Jayson's thick tongue inside of her, she fulfilled another dare and took all of Jayson's length and girth inside of her mouth, stroking him as she did, making him moan, curse, and call her name until he made her stop, rushed to slip on a condom, and positioned himself above her, the tip of his penis poised to part the lips of her pussy.

Jess had let go.

And now her hands were flat against his slick chest, pushing him back, keeping his dick at her door.

Jayson looked at her, his eyebrows furrowed, his eyes dark with disbelief, confusion, and maybe even a touch of anger. "Stop? What do you mean, 'stop'?"

Jess shook her head. "I . . . can't do this, Jayson. This . . . this is wrong."

Still above her, his palms pressed flat on the mattress beside her shoulders, Jayson said, "This isn't wrong, Jess. This is right. You know it. That's why you want to stop. Because you know how right this is."

Jess shook her head again, but hadn't pushed him back any farther, nor had she moved away. "I shouldn't be here," she said, the strength in her voice weaker than before. "I . . . I'm married."

"Unhappily, yes, you are."

"No . . . I'm not."

Slowly, Jayson applied pressure against her arms. "Yes, you are, Jess. You're unhappy, unfulfilled, and neglected." Each word brought with it increased pressure.

"My husband is just busy," Jess said. Her conscience was yelling, its voice at its highest pitch, begging her to straighten her arms, to not let her legs part slowly the way they were, allowing the top of his penis entrance into her shaved wonderland.

"I would never be too busy for you," Jayson said, the tone of his voice deepening. "Every night would be like this night, this moment."

Jess exhaled. She wanted to stop him. She wanted to stop herself. But as much as she didn't want it to, everything felt so, so good. The passion, the intensity, the attention—it had been so long. Too long.

"I'm going to make love to you, Jess," Jayson said softly. "I'm going to fulfill you. I'm going to show you what you can have. I'm going to show you what is yours."

As he talked his chest inched closer to hers, and while that happened, his throbbing member slid farther inside of her.

"I've thought of nothing but being inside of you, Jess. I've dreamed of this moment."

Jess gasped as he pressed his lips against her and plunged deep inside. Jayson moved his waistline to all of the rhythms his tongue had performed to, but with more skill, more passion, and more desire.

Jess dug her fingers into the muscles of his back, and then pulled him down closer, making him go deeper. She moaned as he moved, moving in opposite unison with him, pulling her hips down when he rose up; thrusting upward when he came down.

"Take it, Jess," he said. "It's yours."

"Mine," Jess whispered.

"Yours. All yours."

Jess moaned again.

Jayson thrust in and out harder. "Now . . . tell me, Jess. Is it mine?" He pulled out, then drove back in. "Tell me, Jess. Tell me. Whose is it?" Another pull back, another forceful push back in. "Tell me," he said again. "Whose is it?"

Jess ooh'd. "It . . . it—"

Jayson pulled out, thrust forward, ramming his pelvic bone into hers. "Whose, Jess?" He palmed her ass and held her close as he worked his waistline clockwise.

Jess bit down on her lip and dug her fingers deeper into the crevices of his muscles. "It . . . it's yours," she said, lost in the sex, the fucking that she was experiencing. She pulled Jayson closer and bit harder down on her lip as her waters rose. "Jayson . . . Oh, Jayson!"

Jayson plunged deeper, harder. Jess called his name again. Called out to God. And then her levees broke, and as she called out his name again, an eruption with the force of a tidal wave came crashing down.

"Mine!" Jayson said giving it to her harder, making her orgasm that much more powerful.

He pulled out to his tip. "It's."

He thrust back in as far as she could take him. "All."

He pulled out to his tip again. "Mine!"

He let out a growl, dove back into her, and kept himself deep as he erupted into his condom. He bucked against her as he released himself, and as he did, Jess tried to shed tears. Heavy, fast tears for the breaking of her vows. But while Jayson jerked slowly above her, she couldn't because the regret that she'd felt before Jayson had slid inside of her was gone. Try as she might, there would be no tears.

Seconds later, Jayson rolled off of her and lay on his back, breathing heavily for several seconds. "Wow." He took a few more deep, long inhalations and exhalations to catch his breath before he turned on to his side and faced her. He looked at her, his gaze probing, and said, "Do you want to leave?"

Jess took a slow breath and thought about his question.

Did she want to leave? Did she want to get up, grab her clothes, and run out of there as fast as she could? Did she want to go home and stand beneath a stream of scalding hot water, trying desperately to wash away the shame she should have felt for what she'd done? The right answer had required no words. Just action.

Get up, get her clothes, get dressed, and walk away without looking back.

That was what her answer needed to be. But as right and necessary an answer as it was, it wasn't what she wanted to do.

"I shouldn't be here," she said, her eyes on Jayson. "I'm married. I have a family. I have girls, and it's my job to raise them to never do something like this."

Jayson started to respond, but before he could, she cut him off.

"I shouldn't be here, but I am because I want to be. It's wrong, and I'm probably going to go to hell for it, but denying it would just be a waste of time. I said it before . . . I'm grown."

"Yes, you are. And you have more dares to fulfill."

Jess laughed. Jayson continued to stare at her with intense eyes. It gave her the chills. He leaned forward and pressed his lips against hers, then said, "Have you ever been fucked on a balcony overlooking the city?"

Jess turned her head. Outside of the room, to the right, just past a small sitting area, was a small balcony. She'd noticed it briefly when they were tearing each other's clothes off. She turned back to Jayson and stared at him as he stared back at her with predatory eyes. "Never," she said.

Jayson smiled.

A few minutes later, Jess leaned against the waist-high ledge and admired the view of the city as Jayson took her from behind.

Chapter 26

Jess was grown. She'd said it and meant it. She'd made the decision. It had been wrong, but for a few intense, unforgettable hours, it had been a decision she had needed to make. She'd heard women who'd become caught up in adulterous affairs explain how and why it happened. She'd heard them talk about the *need* factor. The need to be desired. The need to feel beautiful. The need to release. The need to feel like a woman and to be treated as though they were the only woman.

Before Jayson slid inside of her, she had come to fully understand that need because, for so long, she hadn't felt desired, hadn't felt beautiful, and she hadn't had a release. And so when she had her palms flat against Jayson's chest and had told him that she couldn't go any further than they had gone, she'd done so knowing in her heart that she was willingly going to cross the line and let the moment be. It was a choice. A grown-up decision. And she wasn't going to regret it.

But . . .

As she rode the elevator down from Jayson's floor and made her way to her car, regret, guilt, and self-disgust settled down on her so heavily that when she finally made it to her car, got in, and closed the door, she broke down into an uncontrollable fit of tears.

From the moment Jayson slid inside of her, all doubt and apprehension had gone away, but when the elevator doors closed and she found herself alone, the voice of her conscience spoke up and, this time, refused to be silenced.

How could you? You promised him you would always be faithful. You looked into Esias's eyes and vowed the same thing. How are you going to look him in the eye now? How are you going to look your girls in their eyes? Esias is a good man who has always been there for you. He was imperfect when you said "I do." How could you expect him to be perfect now? I tried to warn you. I tried to keep you from doing this, from making this mistake. But you were too selfish to listen. Too caught up in your silly, childish game. Truth or dare. Pathetic!

For nearly an hour, Jess sat behind her steering wheel, crying a waterfall of painful tears as her conscience continued to berate her.

How dare you cry! You talked shit online, and then made a "grown-up" decision to do the wrong thing. No regrets. Remember, you decided that. You decided that being unfaithful was what you wanted to be. No one else. So how dare you sit there and shed tears!

How dare she?

The choice had been hers.

At some point during the chastisement, Jess's well ran dry and the tears ceased to flow. How dare she? It was a valid question. One that she asked herself when she forced herself to stare at her reflection in the rearview mirror.

"You decided," she whispered. "You decided!"

Seconds of silence passed without a reply from her reflection.

"Damn you," she said, slamming her palm against the steering wheel. "Damn you." Her reflection looked back at her, its gaze unapologetic. Jess frowned, said, "Go to hell," and then started her car.

She took a final glance in her rearview mirror, and when she did, her reflection whispered, "You're a hypocrite."

Jess drove in silence, agreeing wholeheartedly.

Chapter 27

Jayson had to have Jess again. And again. And again.

Being with her had been perfect, just like he knew it would be. They were kindred spirits. He was hers. She was his. He had known it before their consummation. He was sure Jess knew it now. "Jess," he whispered.

He breathed in deeply through his nostrils, taking in the scent of her, enjoying the smell of their passion that filled the room.

"Jess."

He hated letting her go, hated giving in when she said that she couldn't stay because she had to get her girls. He wanted to grab hold of her and make her stay with him forever. He almost did. He almost tightened the hold he'd had around her waist when they had been kissing good-bye, and pulled her back into the room. In his mind, he had done that. In his mind, he had pulled her in, pushed her to the bed, locked the door behind him, and then proceeded to ravage her over and over and over again. He wanted to hear her call out his name the way she had when he'd been inside of her. It had sounded so perfect coming from her lips. His name that didn't belong to him.

Jayson whispered her name once more, and then looked at himself as he stood naked in front of a full-length mirror against the wall across from the bed. His blood was pumping as he thought about her. He was sweating from the heat of his thoughts.

"Jesssss."

His father would have been proud.

His cell phone chimed melodically suddenly. Picture mail had come through. He went to his phone, hoping with a smile that the picture was from Jess. A good-bye treat. But his hope and smile quickly fell away when he saw that the mail hadn't been from her.

Regina.

His picture whore.

She'd sent another one. A picture of her pussy with her finger inside of her. In one week there was going to be something else inside of her. Jayson couldn't wait, not because he wanted her, but rather because he just wanted to be done with her. Truth or dare was no fun with Regina because she just sent picture after picture without direction, and that wasn't how the game was played. You didn't just perform without a request being made.

Jayson shook his head as he stared at Regina's perfectly shaved pussy with thick, dark lips, her middle finger halfway inside of it. Nothing about the image aroused him because he hadn't asked for it. He didn't want to add it to her folder because it didn't belong. It didn't have anything to do with the game. He thought about deleting it for a moment, and even brought up the option to do just that. But instead, he changed his mind, chose forward, and sent it to his e-mail. It would be added, and it would be used if she bothered him after he was done with her.

Jayson tossed his phone to the bed and put his focus back on Jess. The woman of his dreams. He looked at himself in the mirror again and imagined touching, caressing, sucking, and moving inside of her in tune, his rhythm matching hers. He inhaled the scent of her again. "Jess."

He grabbed hold of his manhood. Heart and blood pumping, his hand became Jess's and began to move back and forth.

Chapter 28

Fifty thousand dollars. Candy had seen this much money on TV, in the movies and in her dreams, but never in person. It was surreal. It was almost hard to believe what she was looking at, that what lay before her in a black duffel bag on the middle of the plush, queen-sized bed she had been sleeping on for the past several weeks was actually there.

For a split second she just stared at the wrapped greenbacks in the bag, almost afraid to touch them for fear that the money would disappear. But that was only for a split second. Candy, whose name was really Shannon, couldn't keep the smile from spreading across her face as she went to the bed and shoved her hands into the sea of crisp, green paper.

"Half. Just like I promised you. You'll get the other half in a few days. Then you can leave."

Candy stared at the stack of one hundred-dollar bills for a moment, and then looked up at the man who'd given her much more money than she had ever planned on getting from him. Seven weeks ago, he had pulled up to a stop beside her as she stood on the corner that cops avoided, driving a jet-black Jaguar with tinted windows and chrome rims. For a few seconds the car sat idling quietly, its windows remaining up, keeping the driver's identity concealed.

A street-corner prostitute since the age of sixteen, Candy was accustomed to cars pulling up beside her, so that hadn't bothered her, but what had was that the driver hadn't lowered the windows. That just wasn't the way things worked.

After the driver pulled up and lowered the window, she stepped forward, looked into the car with a smile, and said, "You looking for some fun?"

The driver, typically a male, would look at her, sometimes with a nervous expression, other times ravenously, and would respond that he was.

Candy would then open the car door, get in, and say, "Let's go into the alley."

The driver would comply and go into the alley just around the corner. There, Candy would negotiate a fee for her sexual favors. The more involved the service requested, the higher the dollar amount. Once established, money would be placed into her hand, and then whatever the customer wanted, he got.

For ten years that's what Candy was used to. What she wasn't used to was the driver just sitting there, and it made Candy uncomfortable. So much so that she had looked behind her toward the shadows by the alleyway and made eye contact with her pimp, Bishop, who was never far away with his .22. Just as she was about to give him a subtle nod, the Jaguar's passenger window slid down. Minutes later, Candy was sitting in the Jag, parked in the alley, asking the "john" who, by the tension in his body language, had obviously never done anything like that before, what sexual favors he had been looking for.

In ten year's time, Candy had heard it all. Her clients wanted hand jobs and blow jobs. They wanted vaginal penetration and anal sex; they wanted to sit and watch her touch herself while they jacked themselves off. No request surprised her.

Until that night.

"I'm not looking for sex."

"So what are you looking for? You want to watch me play with myself?"

"No."

"Do you want to jerk off and let me watch?"

"No."

Confused, Candy eyed him skeptically, then slid her hand into her purse and closed her fingers around a small can of mace she had concealed inside. "So then, what do you want?" she asked, her grip tight, her arm ready.

His eyes focused through the windshield, the john said, "I want to pay you one hundred thousand dollars to stay with me for as long as I need you. I want you to take pictures of your body. Of you doing things to it—sexual things. I don't want you to ask any questions. I don't want sex. You won't have to worry about food. You'll have a refrigerator stocked with it. You won't have to worry about clothes. There will be outfits for you. You'll have a soft bed to sleep in, cable TV to watch. Say yes and one hundred thousand will be yours guaranteed. Oh . . . and until I'm finished needing you, you won't be able to leave. Do we have a deal?"

Until that night, Candy had never been surprised. But until that night, she'd never been propositioned that way and money like that had never been discussed.

"Are you a cop?"

"No."

Candy took a glance through the windows of the Jaguar. "Am I being pranked? Is this *America's Funniest Home Videos* or something?"

"No and no."

Candy tightened her grip around her mace. "Are you crazy?"

The john shook his head. "No. I just need your services."

"And you're willing to pay me one hundred thousand dollars?" Candy asked, her eyebrows raised skeptically, her lips twisted into a disbelieving smirk.

"Yes, one hundred thousand. If you don't want it, then get the fuck out of my car so I can find another whore who does. If you do, then we leave now."

Candy snapped her head back. It may have been true, but she still didn't like being called a whore. She looked at the man as he watched her with unblinking eyes that seemed almost . . . sad. "You're not fucking with me, are you?" It was a statement, not a question.

"No," he answered his tone flat, no-nonsense.

"One hundred thousand?"

"In cash."

"And you just want pictures?"

"And your silence, yes."

"What do you plan to do with the pictures? Put me all over the Internet?"

The man frowned.

She was irritating him, she could tell.

"You make a living selling your ass and sucking dick for money for far less than what I'm willing to pay you. Do you really give a shit what I do with the pictures?"

Candy raised an eyebrow again, and then took a glance through the tinted window. Bishop was out there watching and waiting for his 90 percent of whatever it was she was going to make. *One hundred thousand,* she thought. Ninety percent was ninety thousand. That was a hell of a lot of money to give up. If the amount was real.

She turned her head and looked at the stranger with the depressed expression. "Are you a serial killer?" she asked.

The man sighed. "If I were, do you think I would tell you?"

Candy stared at him. He stared back, sad and businesslike, waiting for her answer. She didn't know why, but for some reason, she believed him. She took another glance through the tint. Bishop had stepped out of the shadows, no doubt the lack of moaning making him wonder what the hell was going on. Candy turned and looked at the stranger. "My pimp Bishop has a .22. When you drive, you better drive fast and keep your head down."

"So we have a deal?"

Candy thought about it. One hundred thousand dollars. With the percentage Bishop took, she would have to sell a lot of ass and suck a lot of dick to make up that much money. She nodded. "We have a deal. Now drive."

The man put the car in drive and slammed down on the gas pedal. As the car peeled away down the alley, Candy lowered her window, stuck her arm out, and raised her middle finger in the air. Gunshots rang out behind them, and she quickly pulled her arm in and slumped down. Three bullets came through the rear windshield. Candy screamed and threw her hands over her ears. Miraculously, the stranger, who never once bothered to duck low, hadn't been hit.

That was seven weeks ago, when Candy had been prowling the street corners in leather and lace, trying to make enough to keep from being slapped around. Now she was gazing at fifty thousand dollars, cold cash. And it was all hers.

She looked up at her benefactor, whose name she didn't know, as he turned and walked away. In four days, he would give her the other half of her money, and then she could leave. She looked back down at the cash and smiled. For this kind of money, she'd be his prisoner for as long as he wanted.

Chapter 29

Reggie stood in his bathroom and stared into the mirror above the sink and saw the shell of a man that he used to know. A man, who, despite a few extra pounds, had once been fairly handsome. A man who used to shave every day because he hated facial hair and thought it made him look unkempt. This man also used to shave his head bald at least twice a week. This was done to conceal the balding at the crown of his head.

Reggie stared at him. The man in the mirror stared back. He had a seven-week-old beard, and hair sprouting from everywhere but the top. Reggie used to know him. They used to be good friends. But that had been before the heartache and depression.

Reggie looked into the stranger's red-rimmed eyes, eyes that looked as though they hadn't closed in weeks. In four days, the man in the mirror was going to become a killer, and Reggie was going to do nothing to stop him.

Chapter 30

Four days later, Jess sat in front of her laptop with a thudding heartbeat. She was about to do what she knew she had to do the minute she'd broken down in her car before leaving the Gramercy Hotel, the scene of her crime. She was supposed to have done it two days earlier, but she backed out because she'd felt bad.

Before she'd left Jayson's room—although nothing had been set in stone—she and Jayson had spoken about seeing each other again.

"How soon can I see you again?"

"I don't know. Esias doesn't go away often."

"I can come back in two weeks. Do you think you can get out?"

"For a whole night? I doubt it."

"What about a girls' night out? Would he have a problem with that?"

"No. I don't go out much, but I do the occasional ladies' night."

"So let's plan for it."

"We can try."

"You have me hooked, Jess. I don't think I can last longer than two weeks without feeling you again."

"That would be nice."

"So . . . two weeks . . . back here?"

"I can't promise anything, but let me see what I can do."

***

Jess sighed as she turned on her laptop. In a few minutes she was going to tell Jayson that two weeks wasn't going to happen, because it couldn't. Not again. A one-night stand. Technically, that's all their night was. She felt bad about that, not because it was the right thing to do, but rather because Jayson was a good man who didn't deserve to have that done to him. So two days ago, she had backed out and skipped her seminar to avoid him. But now she sat ready and determined to take the first step toward redemption because she needed to be able to look her husband in the eye again. She needed to be able to look at her girls and feel the pride she felt before she'd done the unthinkable. Until she closed the book to a very dark chapter in her life—however short it had been—she couldn't face Esias; she couldn't be her daughters' example. So as Windows loaded, Jess sat still, ready, and desperate to get it over with.

She'd lost herself over the course of seven weeks and as she had, her marriage had suffered. Esias was an imperfect man who was absolutely perfect for her, and for the past few weeks, she had treated him like shit. He didn't deserve that. Her girls hadn't deserved to see the man who loved them more than anything in the world get half-assed treatment.

Jess took a breath, and then moved her arrow to the AOL icon. Jayson would be waiting for her, she knew. She didn't know how he was going to take what she had to say, that after tonight, the game was officially over. But, she couldn't worry about that. The time had come to get back on the right path.

Chapter 31

I can't see u again, Jayson. I'm sorry.

Jayson closed his eyes a bit. The words on his screen glared back at him with the intensity of the summer sun in the midafternoon, shining down without a cloud in the sky to block its rays.

He read Jess's words again, as though reading them would somehow make them go away. But they didn't.

Say something . . . please.

Jayson sat still for a few seconds as his heart began to hammer beneath his chest. This wasn't the conversation he'd expected them to be having. After the night they'd had, the magic, the confirmation that they'd been made for each other, he anticipated them talking about their next time together, and the continuation of the forever that had begun.

She wanted him to say something. Jayson clenched his jaw, then leaned forward and typed. Wht do u wnt me 2 say, Jess?

I wnt u 2 tell me wht ur thinking.

Jayson closed his eyes a little bit more. Wht I'm thnkng . . . He paused, worked his jaw again, and then continued. Wht I'm thnkng is tht u knw wht u jst said 2 me is bullshit.

It's not.

U don't wnt 2 end ths.

I do. I hve 2.

Bullshit.

Jayson ... I can't do ths anymore. I hve a family.

No regrets. Rmembr? U said tht.

I knw I did, but ... but it was naïve of me 2 thnk tht it was possible 2 do smthng so wrong and not regret it.

It wsn't wrng, Jess. It was rght, and u knw it.

I'm sorry, Jayson, but it can't happen again. None of wht we've been doing can.

Ur jst scared, Jess. Ur scared bcuz as much as u wnt 2, u can't deny how rght it is btwn us. This dsn't hve 2 end.

Yes, it does. This is unfair 2 my children and 2 my hsbnd.

Ur not in luv wth him.

Yes, I am.

Ur lyng. Ur in luv wth me, Jess. I saw it in ur eyes.

Jayson—

Leave him and b wth me.

What?

Leave him and b hppy wth me.

I can't do tht. U r crazy.

Crazy in luv ... yeah, jst like u r.

U r a good man, Jayson, and I care abt you, but I'm not in luv wth u, and u r not in love wth me.

Jason cocked an eyebrow at her statement. O no? Thn wht r my feelngs exctly, snce u seem 2 knw?

Lust, Jayson. U r in lust wth me. Tht's all.

Jayson clamped his hand over his head and squeezed his temples with his thumb and index finger. "Lust?" he whispered, the tone of his voice heavy with angered incredulity. Lust?? Wht r u now ... a mind readr?

Jayson ... wht happened between us at the hotl ... the texts and the pics ... it's all been incredible, but none of it had anything 2 do wth luv on either of our parts.

Jayson applied pressure to his temples again. He could not believe she was saying the things she was. He shut his eyes tightly, applied intense pressure to his temples, took a deep breath, and blew it out hard. Then he responded, Now *tht* is defntly sum real bullshit.

We were satsfyng each other's needs, Jayson.

Jayson's mouth dropped open. "Satisfying . . ." he said. He looked at her words with wounded bewilderment, then typed, Wht the fck???

Jayson . . . please . . . dn't do this.

Dn't do wht, Jess?

Dn't get ignorant.

U jst clled me ur fckng maintenance man!

That's not wht I meant and u knw tht.

Not wht u meant? U said I was satsfyng ur fckng needs!

For the last time, Jayson . . . I'm asking u 2 not b ignorant wth me. I dn't mean it tht way.

Jayson slammed a closed fist down on his table. "Bitch!" he yelled out. He typed, U said I satsfied ur needs!!!

U r takng my words the wrng way.

U knw wht, Jess . . . u r a fckng liar.

Excuse me?

The connection we hve isn't abt goddamnd lust. It's luv. I knw it, and u damn well knw it 2.

Jayson—

U luv me.

I'm sorry, but I dn't.

Jayson shook his head. She didn't mean that. U dn't mean tht.

How r u gng 2 tell me wht I do and dn't mean?

The same way u tld me wht I'm really feelng 4 u.

Seconds of tense nonresponse commandeered the heated back-and-forth.

Jayson stared at his screen in disbelief.

A few more seconds passed before Jess responded.

I'm sorry, Jayson. I really am. I didn't mean 4 things 2 go ths way

Jayson scoffed.

U jst ended wht is obvsly the real thing, and thn you clled me a fckng tool. How the fck did u thnk it was gonna go?

I wnted us 2 b friends, Jayson. I'd hoped that it would have been possible. Tht's obviously not going 2 happen. So . . . good-bye.

Jayson sat unmoving, breathing heavily as Jess logged out of AOL. *Love,* he thought. She *was* in love with him. He knew it. She wanted to be with him. No matter what she'd said. She was the yin to his yang, and from the first time they'd chatted, to the first time they laid eyes on each other, to the sex they'd had, the connection between them was obvious and real.

They belonged together.

Jayson flared his nostrils and opened and closed his hands into tight fists over and over as he ground his teeth. *Together,* he thought. He and Jess. Forever. They would be. This was their goddamned time and place. His breathing quickened as did his heart rate as he stared at the words Jess had typed.

Esias.

He must have found out about them and forced her to say those things, because Jayson knew she couldn't have meant them. Not after the things they'd done. There was no way in hell she believed any of the words she'd typed.

Esias.

Jayson was going to let Jess break the news to him. He was going to let her tell him that she was going to leave him to be with the man she was really supposed to be with. But that plan had now changed. Esias was fucking with her head, and it was up to Jayson to see that his bullshit was put to an end. Jess would come around then, when her mind was clear. And, if for some reason her mind remained clouded, he had a folder with her name on it to help clarify things.

His cell phone chimed. Picture mail.

Jayson shook his head and grabbed his phone. Regina again, with another picture. This one a close up of her dark, brown nipple, with a message reading, I can't wait 4 u 2 run ur tongue around ths.

Jayson stared at the picture and felt nothing but rage. For Esias and for Regina. They were fucking up everything. His game. His destiny. They had to be dealt with. Regina first. Then that son of a bitch.

Jayson typed, I'm gng 2 do a lot more than run my tongue arnd it, and then hit send.

Seconds later, Regina responded.

I dare u 2 do tht and more.

O, trust me ... I will.

Mmmm, I'm leaving my front door unlocked. I'll b on my bed naked waiting 4 u.

R u sure u r ready 4 it?

I'm more than ready, baby. I can't wait 4 u 2 gve it 2 me.

Jayson ground his teeth together and as he did, he thought about Jess and her words; words that she'd undoubtedly been coerced into typing. She wanted to be his, all his. And, after he gave Regina more than she bargained for, and after he made Esias disappear, Jess was going to get her heart's desire.

Chapter 32

Reggie tossed his prepaid cell phone to the side and picked up the unregistered .22 he had sitting beside him. He had never fired a gun before. Never even held one—until he purchased it from a street hustler he had approached with three thousand dollars cash. It was more money than had been necessary, he knew, but he didn't care.

He raised the gun up to his nostrils and inhaled its metallic scent. He'd heard people talk about the power they felt with cold steel in their hands, the feeling of invincibility.

He hooked his index finger around the trigger and squeezed it. *"Bang,"* he whispered as tears ran down his face.

He squeezed the trigger again and thought of the moment when an actual bullet would propel from the .22's barrel and sink deep into Jayson's head.

More tears ran down.

His hand remained steady.

He squeezed the trigger one final time. It was going to be a powerful moment.

"Bang."

Chapter 33

Jess closed her laptop, planted her elbows on top of the dining table, and covered her face with her hands. Jayson's reaction had surprised her. She'd expected that he would be hurt and possibly upset by what she'd had to do, but she hadn't been prepared for the vehemence and the biting language.

During her decision-making process, she had thought about telling him face to face that she couldn't go on, but she decided not to because she didn't trust herself to resist the desire to feel him inside of her again. With the ugliness that had come out of him, she was glad that she'd made that decision.

For some reason, she thought she had known Jayson, or at least some of him, but after their exchange, it was obvious that she had never really known him at all, which made her regret what she'd done, even more. But that was over now.

Jess exhaled, releasing with it some of the tension and guilt from her shoulders. Step one was completed. Now step two had to be made. She had to make amends with Esias, not with words, but with actions. She had to give him the love and attention he deserved; something she would do now without Jayson to distract her. She also had to make amends with her daughters. During her slip into darkness, she had been neglecting them also by not paying full attention to their elementary school tales, not taking the time to fully go over their schoolwork the way she usually did, and worse, by rushing them to bed at night when Esias wasn't home so that she would have more time to chat with Jayson.

Jess pulled her hands away from her face and looked around at her home. Toys were scattered around, one or two in the dining and living room, a discarded pair of socks sat balled up in a corner, a T-shirt lay across the arm of a chair, a light film of dust coated some of their cherry-wood furniture and electronics, and the carpet needed to be vacuumed. The toys, the clothing, the dust—they were all minimal, but prior to Jayson's existence, minimal was too much for Jess, who was anal about keeping her house cleaned.

Neglect. It had become her theme for far too long. That was all going to change now.

She rose out of her chair, turned off the light as she walked out of the dining room, and headed upstairs to her daughters' room. Standing in the doorway, she watched them while they slept soundlessly beneath their Tinkerbelle sheets. She felt a pulling at her heart and whispered, "I'm sorry," as a tear escaped from the corner of her eye. "I'm home now."

She watched them for a few more minutes, and then went to her bedroom and stood in the doorway there, and stared at the bed she and Esias shared. She couldn't remember the last time they had made love in it.

She frowned as she looked away from the bed to a framed picture of her and Esias on her night table. It had been taken the previous summer during a picnic in the park. Jess looked at the genuine smiles on their faces, smiles that made it apparent to anyone who viewed them, that no matter what obstacles fell into their paths, they could, and would, conquer them together because they were in love, and they were a team.

She looked back at the bed again, and with a determined nod, promised herself that when Esias got home, she was going to make sure that the bed would be used for more than just sleeping.

Chapter 34

Jayson was there.

Reggie's heart hammered beneath his chest so heavily he found it difficult to take a full breath. He was there; the man who was responsible for his wife's death. The man he had nightmares and wet dreams about.

A chill ran through Reggie as he sat down in a maroon love seat Rita insisted they purchase because it had matched the maroon stitching covering their two bedroom windows that ran from floor to ceiling. He leaned forward, braced his elbows on his knees, and sat motionless for a few seconds. Then he sat back, lay his right ankle across his left knee, his left elbow on the chair's armrest, and remained still for a moment or two before putting his foot back flat on the floor, leaning forward, and resting his elbows on his knees again.

He couldn't get comfortable. His anxiety wouldn't allow it. He was nervous, anxious, eager, fearful, determined, and doubtful, all at the same time. He tried to get himself centered, tried to calm the trembling that had started to overcome him.

He took another half breath. Held it and counted to twenty, and then released the air slowly as the weight of the .22 he held in his right hand increased. He was going to kill Jayson. Without a word, without hesitation. He was going to raise his arm, point the gun, squeeze the trigger, and then watch the man who had sent his wife to an early grave, die.

He had never killed anyone before, and had never thought he would. But life had a way of throwing wicked curveballs, and there had been no more vicious a throw than the day he read his wife's good-bye letter. Nothing could have prepared him for that.

But he was ready now.

Reggie took another breath as he heard the front door downstairs open. His heart began to beat harder, faster. The .22 grew heavier.

You can do this. You have to do this.

Reggie tightened his grasp around the butt of the .22 and, although he had never been very religious, he said a prayer when, a few minutes later, Jayson began to ascend the staircase.

Chapter 35

Regina was waiting for him. Naked. In her bed. She wanted Jayson to walk into her home, come into her bedroom, and fuck her until she was sore. She'd said this in a text she'd sent him, a dare, just before she sent him her address.

Jayson was ready.

He was going to do what she wanted. He was going to make her scream, make her beg him to stop. But he wasn't going to stop. He was going to continue to ravage her, to teach her a lesson for disrespecting the game. For playing out of bounds. She'd taken the desire, the hunger, away. With each unrequested picture, he wanted to violently hurt her more than he actually wanted to sexually hurt her.

He was going to take his anger and frustration out on her. Jess hadn't responded to him. Since her last chat message, she hadn't come back online to class. She hadn't logged on to AOL. She hadn't responded to any of the text messages he'd sent her. All because of Esias. He knew.

That made his blood boil.

Regina was going to pay for the happiness Esias was trying to deny him and the woman he loved, and because of this, he was going to fulfill Regina's dare ten times over. But then she sent her address, and Jayson knew at that moment that Regina wasn't real because Regina's address was Rita's address. And Rita was dead.

Jayson paused at the foot of the wooden staircase he'd ascended once before and looked up. At the top of the staircase, down the hall to the left, in the room at the far end, someone was waiting for him. Someone who he was sure wanted to do him harm.

After the address, he sent a text back telling her to be ready. To be naked with her legs spread wide. He wanted her pussy to be wet and dripping for his dick. She replied back that she would be; that she was already wet. Jayson sent one final text telling her that he was on his way. He waited for her to respond, saying that she couldn't wait before he deleted her file, and then got his gun, a Ruger Mark III Standard, .22 caliber, that he'd purchased from a gun show a few months before. He owned ten different handguns. Glocks, .45s, .357s. He'd used all of them on the target range. He hadn't yet fired the Ruger.

Jayson turned and took a look behind him. He'd already checked to make sure no one had been waiting for him before approaching the staircase, but he wanted one last look anyway.

Jayson turned back around and clicked the Ruger's safety to the off position. Regina, who wasn't, was going to die.

Chapter 36

Candy sat with her fingers clamped around the handles of the black duffle bag filled with half of her money. She was going to get the other half of her payment soon. She just had to wait until her benefactor with the troubled eyes came back down.

She smiled. She didn't know what the man had done with the pictures of her that he'd had her take of herself, nor did she care because the woman that was going to walk away into the sunset with two different duffle bags in her hand wasn't going to be Candy. It was going to be Shannon Hall. The woman that had dreamed of becoming an actress, but who'd never had the money for acting lessons.

Shannon Hall had always dreamed of seeing her name on the big screen. One hundred thousand dollars could get her a great acting coach who would show her how to tap into her raw emotions. With those lessons learned, she could go on auditions and wow casting directors who wouldn't hesitate to give her the starring role. And if, for any reason at all, the director did hesitate, Shannon could certainly suck a mean dick to help convince him.

Candy smiled.

Soon. She just had to wait a little longer.

Chapter 37

Reggie heard the footsteps clicking on his hardwood floor. Easy footsteps. Not light or heavy. Just easy. Relaxed. He imagined Jayson strolling toward the room with a self-satisfied grin on his face. He was coming with the expectation of getting his rocks off. To hell with Regina. To hell with what his "game" would do to her, the emotional effect it would have. Jayson didn't give a shit about her, just like he hadn't given a shit about Rita.

Reggie took a short breath and fought back a tidal wave of raw emotional pain wanting to crash down on him as he thought about the woman he loved unconditionally, despite her infidelity. *No tears,* he thought. *No sadness.* Just rage. Just hatred, disgust, desire. Desire to hurt, to maim, to kill.

No tears.

Reggie tightened his hand around his gun. Its metal butt was warm against the palm of his slick hand. *Kill,* he thought. When Jayson stepped into the doorway, he was going to shoot him multiple times. One shot after the other, until he had no bullets left. There was going to be no thought, no hesitation, no words. He was just going to squeeze the trigger and smile as he watched Jayson die.

Jayson's footsteps grew nearer. Reggie's heart beat harder, faster. In a few seconds it was all going to be over; and then he was going to let Candy, his hired model, go, and somehow, someway, he would find the will to move on.

Jayson's steps grew louder. Reggie took another breath and tried to ignore the sick feeling churning in his gut. A feeling that he wasn't supposed to have.

Fear.

Chapter 38

In four more steps, Jayson was going to be face to face with someone who had outsmarted him. They had walked backward, dropping crumbs as they did, and had watched him shove each morsel into his mouth, as he followed them to the trap they had laid for him. In four steps it could all be over for him. Jayson didn't know what they'd had in store for him, but whatever it had been, Jayson knew that in four steps, they had him.

But then they had fucked up, and now they were going to pay much, much more than Regina was ever going to for making a mockery of his game. Initially, Jayson had been pissed that he could have allowed someone to get the better of him. But the more he thought about it, the more he began to realize that his being outmaneuvered wasn't something to find disgust in, but rather, it was something to learn from. He had been careless, and that was something he couldn't be. His father had never slipped. His father had shown him time and time again how to have his cake and eat it too.

In four steps, before he killed whoever it was that had played him for a fool, Jayson was going to thank them for reminding him that he always had to be on his game.

In four steps.

Jayson took step one with his right foot and took a breath. On step two, he exhaled. His hand holding his Ruger rose with step three. With step four, he stepped into the doorway to Rita's bedroom and saw, just across the room, off to the right, a man pointing a gun at him.

Jayson smiled.

Chapter 39

Reggie stared at Jayson as his heart beat with the force of a hammer coming down on the head of a nail. Jayson. The man who'd submerged his wife in a tub filled with regret and shame. He was holding a gun too.

Reggie steeled himself. He'd never had a gun pointed at him before. His heart rate tripled as he pressed his finger against his .22's trigger. Just a little more pressure and it was going to be over. Jayson was going to be dead. Rita was going to be avenged. Then, and only then, would he allow himself to hate her for what she'd done. Then, and only then, could he let go of the rage he felt, not for Jayson, but for his wife, the unfaithful bitch.

Reggie looked at Jayson as Jayson stared back at him with an amused grin. He had never planned to come and fuck Regina at all. He'd come simply to kill her.

"Looks like we have a Mexican standoff," Jayson said suddenly.

Reggie remained silent as his line of sight went from Jayson's eyes down to his gun, and then back up.

No words. No words!

He applied more pressure to the trigger and waited for the crack of the gun to pierce the air, for Jayson to grunt, to fall down dead. But none of that happened because as much as he tried to, Reggie couldn't seem to will his finger to move anymore.

No!

The pace of his heart increased again as his hand began to tremble ever so slightly.

Do it. Squeeze the trigger.

The thought traveled from his brain stem, but somewhere on its way down to making his finger respond, it got lost and nothing happened.

"You're Rita's husband," Jayson said. "I recognize you from a picture that used to be above the bed. I remember staring at it when I fucked her. It was a good picture, but not nearly as good as the ones you sent me."

Jayson's smile widened, and as it did, Reggie's heart stopped beating for the longest of seconds as the realization of what was happening hit him. Jayson had seen the picture above his bed. The picture that he had taken down and thrown away with all of the other pictures in the house. The house that he had planned on burning down when he was finished.

Jayson had been in his home before.

He was supposed to have been coming to fuck Regina. He was supposed to have been coming to do all of the things he had promised in his dares. But he'd come with a gun instead.

"When you sent the address, I knew Regina wasn't real," Jayson said calmly, as though Reggie weren't pointing a gun at him. "Because this was Rita's address, and I knew Rita was dead. Suicide in the bathtub, right?" Jayson watched him, his eyes dark, his smile twisted.

Reggie swallowed what little saliva he had in his mouth and begged his finger to squeeze the trigger.

He fucked her. My wife. In my bed. She's dead because of him. Squeeze the trigger!

Reggie stared as anger, fear, shock, grief, embarrassment, sadness, and disgust swirled around inside of him. He was emotionally paralyzed, unable to do what had consumed his every thought. He stared, and then opened his mouth.

No! No words. Just do what you want to do; what you need to do! Don't speak!

"Y . . . you killed my wife," he said slowly. The words had escaped before he could reel them in.

Jayson shook his head. "No, I didn't."

Reggie nodded. It was another involuntary action. "Yes . . . yes, you did. You killed her."

"No. I fucked her. Multiple times," Jayson replied coldly. "But when I left her alone, naked in bed with her legs spread wide open, she was breathing."

Reggie's head shook as images he had tried so hard to keep trapped behind a very thin wall began to force their way through. Images of Rita doing things that Candy had done for him. Images of the sex she had said she'd had. The sex that had happened on their bed.

Reggie shook his head again as bile threatened to rise into his throat. "I . . . I'm going to kill you," he said, his throat so thick with grief that the words could only come out in a whisper.

Jayson shook his head. "If you were going to kill me, you would have pulled that trigger already."

"Fuck you," Reggie spat.

Jayson raised an eyebrow. "If I were you, I'd squeeze the trigger before I squeeze mine."

Reggie's chest tightened as Jayson watched him with eager eyes. He looked down to the gun Jayson held in his hand, held his gaze there for a moment, and then looked back up. Squeeze the trigger. That was all he had to do. Squeeze the trigger before Jayson squeezed his.

"You want revenge for your slut of a wife, don't you?" Jayson asked. "Isn't that why you sent me those pictures and messages? Isn't that why you lured me here, to make me pay for fucking her? Pull the trigger and teach me a lesson. I *dare* you."

Reggie could see Jayson's lips moving, but the beating of his heart prevented him from hearing any of his words. Squeeze the trigger. That's all he heard. That's all he wanted to do. There was no need for words. His eyes went back down to the muzzle of Jayson's gun, pointed directly at him.

Before he squeezed his.

Squeeze the trigger.

Reggie thought about it. Willed his finger to react. Just a twitch. That was all it needed to do. A twitch was all the pressure that the trigger was going to need to send a bullet propelling into Jayson's chest.

Sweat trickled down his forehead and down the middle of his back. His heart beat faster, harder.

"Do it," Jayson instructed, his tone even.

Reggie tried. With everything that he had. With all of the desire burning inside of him. With all of the hatred and despair. He tried. But as milliseconds passed, a very painful truth began to encompass him.

He was no killer.

He averted his line of sight down to the gun Jayson held again, then looked back up and stared into Jayson's cold, unblinking eyes. Eyes that were easy to read. Eyes that said that while Reggie couldn't kill, Jayson could.

Reggie took a quick intake of breath; and then he heard a crack. Seconds later, his .22 fell from his hand as he slouched back into the chair while blood seeped out from a hole in his chest.

Chapter 40

He could have died. Right where he stood. A bullet could have hit him in his heart or head, and it could all have been over. Just like it was about to be for Rita's husband.

Jayson stood still and watched him take short, rapid breaths as blood seeped from the gunshot wound in his chest. He was trying to hold on. Trying to fight a battle he couldn't win. The forever sleep was coming, and there was nothing that Rita's husband could do to stop it.

Jayson stared at him with a smirk. He had killed before. Twice. A husband and wife. Tim and Colleen. The Craytons. Their deaths hadn't been planned, but they had been unavoidable.

He had been fucking Colleen anally. It was something she said she wanted. Something that her husband, Tim, wouldn't do to her. It was her dare to Jayson. She wanted to be fucked in her ass while she was choked nearly to the point of passing out. Colleen was a second-grade English teacher with a love for pseudomasochism. During their several chats she had revealed to Jayson how much she enjoyed pleasure and pain, how much it turned her on. She especially enjoyed being choked while she was being penetrated. There was something about the violence of the act, the submissiveness of it that gave her the chills. Before she was married, she had been wild, reckless. Her marriage to Tim had been more of an attempt to settle herself down than it had been for love, and for two years the attempt worked. Sex had become what she'd convinced herself it was supposed to be: clean, and most important, safe. But it was also boring. And, after two years, the freak in Colleen demanded to be released from the closet it had been forced into, and Colleen soon found herself stepping outside of her marriage when the desire to be nasty had been too strong to fight.

Jayson had to kill her because the night he was fulfilling his dare, Tim had come home early from a trip and walked in on them. Tim was six foot four, about 250 pounds, with an attractive smile, who everyone called a gentle giant. Colleen used to complain during their chats about how passive her husband was. How he never got rough during their sex, no matter how much she asked him to. She used to call him a pussy and say that he was so weak that he would probably break down if he ever found out she was unfaithful to him.

She'd been wrong.

Upon seeing them, Tim flew into a rage, and before Jayson could fully pull himself out of Colleen's rear end, the burly man tackled Jayson to the floor and proceeded to hit him with hard blows to his face and ribs. Jayson managed to fend off the brunt of most of the blows with his arms before he managed to turn the tide. Using wrestling techniques he had acquired in the military, he got behind Tim, wrapped his legs with his own, and cut off his airway by holding him in an unrelenting chokehold that eventually snapped Tim's neck. Killing Tim hadn't been his intent, but once he began to squeeze, he found himself unable to stop.

Already hysterical, Colleen's yelling intensified into an uncontrollable outpouring of tears and screaming. Jayson tried to get her to calm down, to listen to him as he explained how he'd had to defend himself, but no matter how hard he tried, Colleen wouldn't shut her mouth. She kept screaming, moaning, sobbing, kept calling him a murderer. His adrenaline already on overdrive, the more Colleen wailed, the more frustrated Jayson became until, without a thought, he wrapped his fingers around her throat and squeezed until screaming would be something she would never, ever do again.

The event should have rocked Jayson to his core. After all, he had just killed two people in cold blood—something he had never done before. But it hadn't. In fact, instead of shaking him and putting him on edge, the violent act seemed to calm his nerves so much that for several minutes, he stood stoic and just stared down at the husband and wife that would forever be united.

He stared just as he was doing now, watching Rita's husband take his last breath.

When he had killed Colleen and her husband, he had been unprepared, so he'd had to get rid of all evidence of his existence, which he had by dousing their bodies with gasoline he found in their garage, and setting them on fire. He flexed his fingers around his Ruger. His hands were covered by latex gloves. This time, he didn't have to worry about leaving behind traces of himself.

He looked at Rita's husband for a few more seconds, and then walked over to him. "Your wife was a whore," he said, making sure not to get too close as Rita's husband was spitting up blood. "But, damn, she was a good fuck."

Rita's husband looked at him through terrified eyes that were dimming with each passing second.

"You should have pulled the trigger," Jayson said. He took one final, long gaze at the dying man, and then turned and walked away. Colleen's husband had intended to kill him. And so had Rita's. Both times he had survived, and as he walked out of Rita's home, he knew why.

He got into his Escalade, closed the door, grabbed his cell phone, and pulled up a picture from his photo album; a picture of Jess, naked from the waist up, holding her breast for him.

Jayson smiled as one word ran through his mind: Destiny. He and Jess, destined, meant to be. That's why death had been unable to claim him, because there was no getting in the way of destiny.

Jayson put the phone down inside of his cup holder and started his engine. The time for games had come to an end. It was time for destiny to be fulfilled.

Chapter 41

A crack. Coming from upstairs. The sound of it had been faint, but Candy had no doubt about what it had been: a gunshot.

She stood still, breathing slowly as her heart rate increased. She had been leafing through half of her easy money, waiting for her benefactor to come and give her the rest, and then let her go when she'd heard the sound of the front door open and close. At first, she wondered if her benefactor had left, something he hadn't done since he had brought her to his home, but then she heard footsteps moving around on the floor above her after the door had closed. In the eight weeks she had been living as a well-paid prisoner in the moderately furnished basement, she had gotten to know the steps of the stranger with the sad eyes. He walked slowly and heavily the way someone usually did first thing in the morning. In the seconds after the front door closed, she knew right away that someone had come into the house because the steps moving around on the hardwood floor had been light and easy, almost casual.

The knowledge of someone else being present put her on edge. Who was the person? What had that person come for? Had he or she known she was there? Had someone come for her? Her heart beat heavily as she stood to the side of the wooden door leading to the upstairs that her benefactor always kept locked.

She stood stoically with a table lamp clutched in her hand, ready to be used like a baseball bat or hammer if someone other than the benefactor came downstairs. Seconds turned into minutes as the footsteps moved around before they disappeared. She hadn't heard the front door open and close again, so Candy had known that whoever had come inside hadn't left, which meant that someone must have gone upstairs.

Candy remained by the door and was going to stay there until whoever had come inside decided to leave. But then she heard the gunshot. A few minutes after that, she heard the light, easy footsteps again before the front door opened and closed once more.

Candy breathed slowly and waited for ten minutes to pass after the footsteps disappeared; and then she waited for another ten minutes before she wrapped her right hand around the doorknob. Someone had come in, a gunshot had gone off, that someone walked away, and now there were no sounds; she had to get out of there. She tried the knob, but it didn't turn. Her heart began to beat harder, faster. She needed to get out! She put the lamp down on the floor, and then put both hands around the knob and tried again, knowing the result would be the same.

Working the streets for as long as she had, Candy had come across and survived many different types of situations, so rarely did anything cause her to panic. But this was a situation she had never been in, and as the doorknob refused to give, panic, along with regret, began to set in. "Dammit," she whispered.

She tried rattling the knob again for no good reason, and then stopped and placed her forehead against the door and sighed. "Dammit," she whispered again.

She shook her head, and then stepped back away from the door and looked up at the ceiling. No sound had come from above for over twenty minutes. Candy opened her mouth, hesitated for the briefest of moments, questioning what she was about to do, and then yelled out, "Hey!"

She waited for a moment, and when no response came, she yelled out again. "Hey! Is someone up there?"

Again silence.

She went back to the door, closed her fist, and pounded on it. "Hey! Are you there? Let me the fuck out!"

She beat on the door again, yelled out once more, then kicked at it. It was all futile she knew, but she was scared. She turned and looked toward the small room she'd been staying in, and stared at the black duffel bag sitting on the bed. Fifty thousand dollars, right there.

She turned back to the door, and then looked back at the money; her money for the taking. She faced the door again. She had only one option.

She took a few steps back, took a breath, and then, just like a football player did on the field, she charged forward and threw her shoulder into the door. The door didn't swing open, but she had rammed into it hard enough for her to realize that another two or three charges, and it was going to give way.

She took another breath, blew it out heavily, said to hell with the ache in her shoulder, and threw herself into the door again, and again. Then, one more time before she fell forward to the ground as the door swung open. She remained silent on her knees and listened to see if anyone had been coming. After a few short seconds of silence, she stood up, grabbed her duffel bag, and made her way cautiously upstairs into the kitchen. There she stood unmoving as her heartbeat hammered so hard beneath her chest, she could hear it above the silence.

Silence. Nothing but.

Candy took another breath, held it for a couple of seconds, and then exhaled slowly. She thought about the silence, and about the fact that the light and easy footsteps had come and gone, while the heavy and slow steps had been nonexistent now. Then she thought about the gunshot. She tilted her head upward and looked up.

Leave, Candy. Take your fifty thousand and leave now before someone comes.

Candy tightened her grasp around the duffel bag.

Go! You don't need to go upstairs. You don't need to go and see what happened.

Candy took a breath again. Held it as her heart pounded. Leave. That was what she needed to do. Leave. Don't walk. Run.

She exhaled, and then made her way through the kitchen, which was empty save for the stove, dishwasher, and refrigerator, and stepped into a large but empty living room. Candy looked around. No furniture, no pictures. *Odd.* To the right of the living room was the dining room, which held a long dining table with one chair at its head. *Odd,* Candy thought again. She moved through the living room and stepped into the foyer, which had white marble flooring and a staircase leading upstairs. The front door was off to the right. Her freedom.

Candy looked at the door. *Go straight to it,* she thought. *Go to it, open it, and get away with your money. Ignore the staircase.*

She took a step forward. She heard the instructions loud and clear as though they'd been given over a loudspeaker. Loud, clear, specific. Instructions not to be ignored. Yet, still, she took more steps forward, not toward the front door, but, rather, to the staircase where she put her hand on the banister and began to make her way upstairs.

Turn around. Go! Someone could be there waiting for you. Take the money and go!

Candy ignored the warning. She continued slowly, cautiously, to the top. Then she took tentative steps down the hallway, past two empty bedrooms, to the master bedroom, where what she saw caused her to take a quick breath of air through her mouth, which had dropped open.

Slumped back in a small maroon love seat, his head tilted back, the front of his blue button-down shirt soaked bright red with blood. Her benefactor. Shock and fear paralyzed Candy for several seconds. Her eyes fixated on the blood soaking his shirt. Blood released because of the gunshot she had heard.

"Oh my God," she whispered, then jumped when the bloody body began to cough. She inched into the room, her eyes focused not on the blood, but the very slow rise and fall of his chest. He was alive.

"H . . . h . . . hel . . . he . . . lp."

Candy looked up. His eyes barely open, the benefactor was looking at her.

"He . . . hel . . . p . . . ple . . . ple . . . ase . . ."

Candy swallowed bitter saliva that had gathered in her mouth, and then gently put her duffel bag down.

The benefactor lifted his arm slowly and pointed toward his bed. "Pl . . . plea . . . m . . . my ce . . . ll . . . it . . . it's th . . . ere . . ."

Candy looked at the bed. Sitting in the middle of the mattress was his BlackBerry, along with a set of keys, one of which was connected to a remote to lock and arm his car.

"Pl . . . lease c . . . call . . ."

Candy looked back at the man. His chocolate-brown skin was paling, and she knew that if there was any chance at all to save his life, she had to make the call right away. She took a step, and then paused as something caught her eye. She looked down to the floor at the foot of the bed and saw a black handle similar to the one on her duffel bag.

Her heart skipped a beat.

She looked down at her bag, to its handle, then looked back to the one sticking out from beneath the bed. Same color, same texture, same size.

She looked to her benefactor as he began to cough again. He had promised to pay her the other half of her money after whatever it was that he'd been doing was done. Then he was going to let her go.

Candy looked back at the handle and moved forward, bent down, and wrapped her fingers around it. She pulled it from the bed, a duffel bag identical to the one he had already given her. Her heart racing now, she lifted the full bag onto the bed, unzipped it, and smiled as she stared at the other half of her payment.

"I . . . I . . . ha . . . have mo . . . more . . ." her benefactor whispered. "J . . . just . . . pl . . . lease . . . c . . . call . . ."

Candy looked at the cash, inhaled the scent of it, and turned and looked at the other bag. Fifty plus fifty. One hundred thousand dollars. Right there, as promised. Now he was promising more.

She looked at him. His skin was paler than before. Beads of sweat ran down his forehead. Blood trickled from the corner of his mouth, and the stain on his shirt had widened.

"Pl . . . pleas . . ." he pleaded again, his voice growing weaker.

Candy looked from him to his BlackBerry, to the money in the bag, to the keys beside his cell, and then back to him. He had more. She just had to make the call. But calling meant bringing the paramedics, and more important, the police. If there was any one group of people Candy hated dealing with, it was the boys in blue, unless they were paying, which many on her corner had. But her corner was no more because she didn't need to deal with it anymore. Not with one hundred thousand dollars.

She stared at her benefactor, whose sad eyes had dimmed even more. Death was coming for him. More. It would have been nice to have. But staring at him, she knew that no call was going to keep the inevitable from happening.

Candy shook her head slowly as she zipped the duffel bag shut and closed her fingers around the handle. "I'm sorry," she said as she reached toward the middle of the mattress with her free hand and grabbed the keys. "I'm sorry," she said again, backing away.

Her benefactor coughed, spat blood, pleaded, "Pl . . . plea . . . se . . . do . . . don't . . ."

Candy frowned, shook her head, and then with barely a pause, turned, bent, and grabbed the other duffel bag. She hurried out of the room, the house, and into a Mercedes Benz sitting in the driveway.

Forty-five minutes later, after giving the keys to the Benz to a group of street-corner thugs, she sat in the last seat on the back of a Greyhound Bus heading to California. With one hundred thousand dollars, Shannon was going to find the best acting coach money could buy. Candy was no more. She'd left her behind with her benefactor.

Chapter 42

Two Months Later . . .

Esias was tired. His body was tired; his eyes wanted to close and stay closed, at least for more than three hours. But, as badly as he wanted to, he just couldn't sleep because he was too close to achieving his dream. It was just within his grasp. The opportunity of a lifetime. Two months ago, his boy had played one of the tracks he'd done for his cousin, who then played the track for Mary J. Blige, who he knew personally, who then relayed, through the cousin, who passed it on to Esias's boy, who then told Esias that Mary was very, very interested in hearing a lot more of what he had and wanted to set up a meeting with him when she finished the short European tour she was on.

Mary J. Blige. The queen of hip-hop soul!

Esias's body was tired, but his mind was energized. In two weeks, he would be flying to LA to meet with Mary and her manager to play for her all of the tracks that he had tirelessly been working on. His hard work was about to pay off. He could feel it. Life was going to change for him and Jess and the girls. Everything just had to be perfect. The lows, the highs, the tempo, the synchronization, the levels. Perfect. There would be no second chance; he knew that. So, as tired as he was, as much as he just wanted to go home after a hard day's work, grab the remote, and kick his feet up, rest was not allowed.

Esias ran his hand down over his face as he rose from behind the mixing board. He'd had three cups of coffee and a Red Bull; he needed to take a piss. He ran his hand down over his face again and scratched on the stubble of hair on his cheeks, musing to himself how quickly hair grew back just after one day. He yawned, stretched up on his toes, and whispered, "Sleep is over-rated." He chuckled. His partner Daren had disagreed and had gone home when the clock struck twelve. Esias called him Cinderella. Daren simply nodded and stated that he was proud to be.

Esias shook his head and smiled thinking of their banter as he stepped out of Studio B and made his way down the very quiet and empty corridor, heading to the bathroom. Standing in front of the women's restroom door with his supply cart was the maintenance guy, Teddy. An older gentleman with a healthy paunch in his midsection and a thick beard, peppered with specks of grey, Teddy had been doing night duty in the studio for the past two months. Esias said a soft, "What's go-ing on?" as he passed the stocky man. Teddy, looking down at the cleaning supplies attached to the cart, kept his head down and gave a nod. He never spoke. As Es-ias walked by him and stepped into the men's room, he wondered if Teddy were mute.

Esias walked by dirty mirrors on his way to the urinal and paused momentarily to glance at himself. "Over-rated," he said staring briefly at eyes lined with dark cir-cles. He shook his head and went to relieve himself, the urge to pee getting stronger. "Come on," he said, as his zipper refused to go down. He fiddled with it, and as he did, the bathroom door opened and closed. Esias took a quick glance over his shoulder to see Teddy walking in with the cart behind him. No nod this time, he turned back around and put his attention back on his reluctant zipper. "Come on," he said, the urgency increasing. "Finally," he breathed as the zipper became unstuck and went down.

He began to reach into his boxer-briefs to fish his penis out, but before he could, a hand cradled the back of his head and shoved him forward, sending him face-first into the wall in front of him. Seconds later, as blood flooded from his nose, Esias fell backward to the floor, where the back of his head hit hard on the floor's linoleum tiles.

He groaned as the room began to spin and fade in and out of darkness. He blinked several times, trying to clear his head, but that did nothing but produce spots before his eyes. He was falling into unconsciousness he knew. He tried to turn over in an attempt to stand, but he couldn't get his arms to respond to his thoughts. Esias blinked and took a breath through his mouth, as he couldn't through his nose, which he knew had been broken, along with several jagged teeth he could feel against his tongue. He blinked and coughed, the action making the pain in his head hurt worse, and moaned again.

The darkness began to overtake the light before him as he lay on his back. His eyes closed, remained that way for a few seconds, and then opened. When they did, standing above him, staring down at him . . . was Teddy.

That, and the warmth of his own urine running down his leg, would be the last thing Esias would remember as he fell into blackness.

Chapter 43

Ringing.

Jess heard it, but she was far away in a cabin ablaze with light from firewood burning in the fireplace. Soft music played from speakers that couldn't be seen. Shadows danced on the walls to the sensuous rhythm of the music that seemed to fit into no specific genre. It was just slow, erotic, rhythmic; perfect for the love-making taking place between Jess and her husband as they sat on the cabin floor, naked with just a blanket around their waists.

Jess moaned as she rode Esias in slow, melodic time to the tune being played. She leaned her head back, closed her eyes, smiled, and clenched her teeth as Esias drove himself deeply up into her, while she bore down on him, helping him along. She moaned. Called his name. Told him that she loved him. Him and only him. She called his name again. Begged, *demanded* he go deeper, harder, faster. She cursed and told him that he had reached her spot and that he shouldn't stop.

The music swelled as Esias did. The climax was build-ing, the tempo rising. Jess moaned louder. Felt tears of ecstasy run down her cheeks as she began to quiver deep inside.

And then the ringing started. Faint and distant at first, but growing louder with each subsequent shrill.

Jess opened her eyes. The music was gone. There was no fireplace, no flames to cast light, no shadows dancing on the walls. She wasn't in the cabin, but her bed, fully clothed and, as she looked to Esias's empty side, alone. She sighed, turned her head, and looked at the time displayed on the alarm clock on her night table beside her. Two o'clock in the morning. *Where was he?*

She reached toward the corner of the night table, grabbed the cordless phone making too much noise, hit the talk button, said, "Hello?" and waited for her husband to explain why he hadn't come home yet.

"Hi, Jess."

Jess's heart beat so heavily, it stole her breath away. The voice belonged not to Esias, but instead, to someone she hadn't heard from for a month and a half. She sat up. "J . . . Jayson?"

"Jess."

"H . . . how did you get this number?"

On the other end, Jayson took a breath and let it out as a heavy sigh. "I left you a ton of messages, Jess. I sent texts, voice mails. I sent you pictures of what I know you wanted. But you never replied."

Jess sat up. "I told you, Jayson . . . what happened was a mistake."

"I blamed Esias at first, Jess. I kept telling myself that he was responsible for you not texting or calling me back. That he must have found out about us and had gotten jealous about how real our love was and forced you to ignore me."

Jayson's call had her shaken, but it also had her angry. "How the hell did you get this number, Jayson?" she asked again. "I never gave you this number."

Jayson sighed into the phone again. "How doesn't really matter, Jess. What does matter is that I was wrong. I was pissed at Esias when I really should have been pissed at you."

A chill ran through Jess. The tone in Jayson's voice was becoming thicker, deeper with anger. She looked toward her bedroom door and wished for Esias to come walking into the room. *Where is he? Why isn't he home yet?*

She tossed her bedsheet off of her, got out of the bed, and went to her dressing table. Her cell phone was there in a charging station she'd bought at Staples.

"You could have called me, Jess," Jayson continued. "You could have texted me. You had time. You could have done it in the morning when Esias pulled away from your town house in his Toyota. You could have called me back while you sat in the bumper-to-bumper traffic each morning instead of yakking away on the phone to someone else."

Jess stood frozen with her cell in one hand and the house phone gripped tightly in the other while she held it firmly against her ear for a moment. Then, she went to the bedroom window and carefully lifted one of the horizontal slats of her blinds and looked out into the parking lot of her development that was dimly lit by a solitary street lamp. She searched for any cars she didn't recognize or anyone that may have been lingering around, but she saw nothing aside from the usual.

He'd mentioned her town house, Esias's Toyota, the bumper-to-bumper traffic she dealt with every morning. Never once in all of their chats had she ever mentioned her house, never once had she ever told him what type of car Esias drove, and never once had she ever complained to him about the frustrating morning rush-hour traffic.

Never.

Jess let the blind close, backed away from the window, and let the house phone drop to the floor. She looked back toward the window and shook her head.

Then she took a few more steps backward and stood still in the middle of her bedroom.

Esias. Where was he?

She raised her cell, found the last number dialed, and hit send and waited for her husband to reply. One ring became two. Two became three. Three turned into four and five before his voice mail answered. "Dammit," she whispered. She left him a message telling him to get home right away, and then sent him a text message, telling him the exact same thing with a 911 at the end. She tried calling him again and still only received his voice mail. "Dammit, Esias."

Then she suddenly heard a buzzing sound. Short, robotic buzzing with barely a pause. It was the tone letting you know when your phone was off the hook. She looked down to the ground, at the phone she'd dropped.

Jayson was gone.

She moved to it, clicked end to hang it up and was about to call her husband again when it rang, causing her to jump. She looked at the caller ID and let out a relieved sigh as Esias's cell number was displayed. She hit the talk button and pressed it against her ear. "Esias! Oh God! Where are you?"

"That hurts, Jess."

Jess pulled the phone away from her ear and checked the number on the ID, reconfirming that it had been Esias's number she had seen.

Her heart already racing with the speed and strength of a jackhammer, it began to beat even harder and faster. So much so that she found it difficult to breathe.

"I sent you so many texts, Jess, and not once did you respond to me, but here you go sending him one."

Jess shivered. He was calling from Esias's phone. "Wh . . . where's my husband?"

"Esias is tied up right now. Literally."

"What . . . what have you done to him?"

"Nothing, Jess. Nothing at all. Not yet anyway."

Jess shook her head. "Let me speak to him."

"Sorry, but that's not going to happen."

Another wave of chills passed over her as anger began to well up inside of her. "Goddammit, Jayson, let me speak to my husband."

"I already told you no, Jess. Now . . . for Esias's sake, don't ask me anymore."

Jess's stomach twisted into knots. "What, goddammit! What is it going to take to make you stop?"

"Honesty, Jess. Your honesty. That's what I want."

"What . . . what do you mean? What honesty?"

"I want you to admit what I know is the truth. I want you to admit to me that you want to be with me."

"I don't want that, Jayson."

"Why do you insist on lying, Jess? Why do you insist on trying to deny the obvious?"

"I'm sorry you don't believe me, Jayson, but I'm not lying."

"Bullshit!" Jayson yelled out into the receiver. "That's bullshit, and unless you want something to happen to Esias right now, you'll stop with it and tell the goddamned truth!"

Jess shook her head. She couldn't believe this was happening, didn't want to believe it, didn't want to accept that what was happening was possible, yet she was forced to accept the reality that she had in some way, though perhaps not to this extreme, seen this coming. The signs for his becoming obsessed had been there when he'd gone off after she had ended the game during their last chat and even more so when he had relentlessly sent her text messages and pictures. But then everything had stopped, and as each day of Jayson's sudden disappearance passed, she began to let her guard down more and more, and allowed herself to think that her foolishness was going to be able to remain hidden behind her steel door.

And now Jayson had her husband.

"I am telling you the goddamned truth, you son-of-a-bitch!" she screamed out. "I don't want you. I never did!"

"Why, Jess? Why do you keep lying to me? All of our chats and pictures and texts. The sex between us . . . you felt the connection."

"It was all meaningless, you asshole!" Jess had tried to keep herself together—especially for her husband's sake—but the more Jayson spoke, the more regret and fear fueled the anger inside of her. "None of it meant anything!"

"Shut up, Jess, before I kill Esias right now! Shut up!"

Tears began to fall slowly from Jess's eyes as she pressed her lips together. Stop. Calm down. She had to. "Please," she said, trying to subdue the harsh tone in her voice. "Please just let him go. I . . . I'm begging you," she asked, her voice barely audible.

Silence was Jayson's reply for several seconds before he said, "Meet me at our hotel in two hours, Jess. Same floor. Same room. I want you to look me in the eye and tell me that you feel nothing for me."

"And when I do? Will you let him go? Will you leave us alone?"

"You won't do that, Jess, because you won't be able to. You'll see. Now . . . two hours. And Jess . . . for Esias's sake, make sure you come alone and don't even think of calling the police."

Jayson ended the call, leaving Jess with nothing but heavy silence.

Angry tears ran, and as a shiver crept up from the base of her spine, she threw her house phone against the far wall.

Chapter 44

Jayson slid Esias's phone closed and slammed it down on his passenger seat. His heart was hammering beneath his chest as his hands shook. He looked up into the rearview mirror of his SUV and stared at Esias, who was propped up in the backseat bound with duct tape around his wrists and ankles and pressed over his mouth. His eyes were wide with fear and confusion. Jayson had waited for him to regain consciousness before he made the call to Jess. He wanted to make sure that Esias heard the conversation. He wanted Esias to understand that Jess was going to be his, and that nothing and no one was going to keep that from happening.

"She was lying," Jayson said, watching him. "She felt the connection. That's why she kept chatting with me when you weren't around. That's why she sent pictures, and then let me slide inside of her. She and I belong together, and she knows it, and when she sees me later, she's going to admit that. You won't be privy to that conversation though, because you're going to be dead by then." He stared long and hard at Esias as Esias stared back at him.

"Jess is distracted because of you. She knows she's supposed to be with me and she wants to be, but as long as you're around, her mind is cluttered with confusion, and she can't think or see clearly. I need for her to be able to because she and I have a family to raise. So

. . ." Jayson paused, raised his eyebrows and shrugged as he sucked in both lips. ". . . you have to go. But I don't want you to worry. I'm going to take good care of her. I'll take care of your daughters too. I'll raise them as my own. I'll even let them call me Daddy."

From the backseat, despite his bindings, Esias lashed out and mumbled harshly from behind the duct tape.

"What was that?" Jayson asked. "I can't understand you."

Esias mumbled again, louder, harder, his mumbled tone as angry as the look in his eyes.

Jayson shook his head. "Are you threatening me?"

Esias slid down in the seat, lashed out with his bound legs, and kicked the back of Jayson's seat as his mumbles and nodding head stated that he was, indeed.

Jayson turned around in his seat and aimed his Ruger, which he'd been holding in his lap, at Esias's chest, prompting immediate silence and stillness. Jayson watched him as he stared at the Ruger's barrel, his chest heaving up and down as he breathed heavily.

"She was never yours," Jayson said. "She was just on loan to you until destiny had a chance to catch up to us. And now that it has . . ." Jayson turned back around, opened his car door, stepped out, moved to the back passenger door, and opened it. His Ruger leveled at Esias's chest, he grabbed hold of Esias's arm and dragged him out of the car to the ground. "Now that it has," Jayson said again, "your time is up."

Unable to move, Esias lay on the hard concrete of a dimly lit alleyway littered with trash and empty cardboard boxes. Esias looked up at him, shook his head, and began to mumble again. He was pleading for his life, Jayson knew. He could tell by the way he was moaning. He could see the fear and desperation in his eyes.

Jayson smiled with sinister amusement, then looked up as a siren screamed from somewhere in the distance. An ambulance. Jayson listened and idly thought about Reggie. He'd seen on the news that Reggie's body had been discovered two days after his death by a friend who had become worried about him when her phone calls had gone unanswered and her messages unreturned. She'd gone to the house to check on him and saw that his car was missing but his front door was slightly open. Reggie's death was being considered a robbery/homicide. Jayson had found the article very interesting.

As the sound of the siren faded away, Jayson looked back down in time to see Esias's chest deflate and his head, which had been lifted, drop back down to the dirty concrete.

"This is destiny, Esias. Your life is about to end. Mine and Jess's are about to begin. Nothing and no one's going to come to your rescue and stop that."

Tears beginning to fall slowly from the corner of his eyes, Esias begged for his life in mumbles again.

Amused by the sight of his groveling, Jayson watched him for a few seconds, and then casually sent a bullet into his chest. "Destiny," he said. "It can't be stopped."

He turned, climbed back into his Escalade which he'd left idling the entire time, slipped it into gear, and with a single glance in his side mirror at his distraction now removed, pressed on the gas and drove away. He never noticed the teenager that had been hiding behind a Dumpster just off to his left.

Chapter 45

Shane Mitchell thought for sure he'd been caught. He had tried to turn into an alleyway and duck behind a Dumpster, but when the jet-black Escalade pulled to a stop a few feet away from where he'd hidden, he was positive that he hadn't been quick enough. His heart beating like a heavy bass drum, he cursed himself for sneaking out to see his girlfriend Traci from math class. Traci had promised him they would go all the way this time, and because Shane was the only virgin in seventh grade, he was determined to make sure that Traci kept her word. He was tired of lying and talking the talk. He wanted to walk it now. So he snuck out, despite having been caught just a couple of weeks ago by his mom who literally beat him for a few days, and climbed the fire escape leading up to Traci's third-floor bedroom window, and snuck into her room. Ten minutes into the action he had been praying for, there was a heavy bang against her bedroom door. Thankfully, Traci had locked it or for sure Shane would have been a goner as Traci's stepfather bellowed that he knew she wasn't alone and demanded to be let into the room.

Wasting no time, Shane threw his clothes on and hustled out through the window. Halfway down the fire escape, Traci's stepfather screamed out from above him, promising to catch and kill him. Shane ran as fast as he could and when he realized there was a car approaching in the distance behind him, he made his

move to the alleyway, and then behind the large metal
bin that reeked of rotting garbage.

For a split second he thought he was safe, but then
the Escalade pulled into the alley where it sat idling for
a few minutes before the passenger door opened. Shane
nearly pissed on himself as a tall guy wearing dark blue
jeans, a grey sweater, and black boots stepped out of the
car with a gun in his hand. On the verge of tears, Shane
was about to step out from his hiding spot and plead for
his life, when the guy with the Maxwell hairdo moved to
the passenger door, opened it, began speaking, and then
dragged another guy who'd been bound and gagged with
duct tape out onto the concrete.

Unmoving, and breathing as slowly and silently as
he could, Shane watched as the brother with the gun
said something about destiny, and then shot the other
guy in the chest before getting back into his ride and
driving away. He'd seen people get shot before on TV
and in movies, but in real life the act wasn't nearly as
dramatic.

Shane sat still for a few minutes. Only when he was
certain that the shooter wasn't going to come back
did he finally and very cautiously emerge from behind
the Dumpster and make his way over to the bleeding
victim who was lying deathly still. He thought about
touching the body, and made a move to do so, when the
man's eyes suddenly fluttered open.

"Shit!" Shane yelled out, stumbling backward and
falling onto his rear end. He remained there frozen,
his heart racing as though he'd just run for his life all
over again, and watched as the man who wasn't dead
at all move slightly and moan softly. Shane whispered,
"Shit," again, and then swallowed saliva that had
formed in his throat. He took a glance in the direction
of the SUV that was long gone, and then inched closer
to the wounded man. "Dude," he said. "Y . . . you OK?"

It was a stupid, stupid question he knew, but he was freaked out and that had been the first thing that he could think to say. He shook his head, called himself an idiot, then looked at the guy whose eyes fluttered open and closed. And then his cell phone vibrated in his pocket. Shane yelled out again. He had forgotten about his cell.

His heart hammering now, he dug into his pocket, pulled it out, and then groaned. His mother, calling. His shoulders dipped as his chin dropped to his chest. "I'm dead," he said with a sigh.

Dead.

He looked from his phone to the guy on the ground, the guy who wasn't dead. Yet. Shane looked at him, and then looked back at his cell. Whether he did the right thing or not, there would be no escaping his mother's wrath for disobeying her. He shrugged, ignored his mother's call, and then dialed 911. Death for him was inevitable. He may as well go out a hero.

Chapter 46

"You have to call the police, Jess."

Jess shook her head. She was sitting at her kitchen table, dressed in jeans, a grey hoodie, and white Nike's on her feet. Her hair was uncombed and hidden beneath one of Esias's Pittsburgh Steelers caps. Her friend Melissa sat across from her, staring at her with imploring eyes.

Jess removed the hat, ran her hands through her hair, and shook her head. "I can't," she said, her voice soft. Her girls were upstairs sleeping, and she wanted to make sure they stayed that way. Her oldest had walked into the bedroom just after she had thrown her phone against the wall. Jess told her the phone had slipped from her hand, and then carried her back to bed.

"But Jess—"

"He said he would hurt Esias if I brought anyone, Melissa. I can't."

Jess had called Melissa with her voice cracking and tears flowing after her conversation with Jayson, and had asked her to come over right away. Melissa had wanted to know what had been wrong, but Jess was too distraught and told her she would explain everything when she arrived, which she had in detail.

Hearing the sound of her voice recount everything that she had done made the pain of what was happening now sting even more. She'd been selfish, and her deceit and betrayal had now put the man she loved with all of her heart, the father of the girls who adored him, in danger. Jess wanted to scream and only to keep from disturbing the girls did she manage to keep from doing just that.

She covered her face with her hand. "Christ," she said softly.

Melissa reached across the table and put her hand over Jess's. "Honey, you need to go to the police. You can't go and meet him alone."

Jess shook her head again and pulled her hand away. "Dammit, Melissa . . . I told you I can't take the chance. I have to go alone."

"Not calling the police or going there alone doesn't guarantee that Esias is going to be safe, Jess. I know it's hard to hear this, but for all you know, something may have already happened. I mean, he was using Esias's phone."

Jess gave her Greek friend a stern glare. "Melissa, I called you because I need your help and support."

"And you have it, honey."

"Then, please do me a favor and stop putting negative energy out there."

"I'm not trying to be negative," Melissa said with a frown. "I'm just trying to keep it as real and as honest as I think a friend should do. I know you've thought about what I said, whether you want to admit it or not."

"Melissa, please . . . please just stop."

Melissa shook her head. "You need to call the police, Jess. If you don't, then I'm sorry, but I will."

Jess looked at her friend. "You wouldn't," she pleaded more than said.

Her eyes unapologetic, Melissa said, "Yes, I will, Jess. I'll have to."

"Please," Jess said. "I'm begging you . . ."

"Jess—"

"Dammit, Jayson promised to hurt him if I told or brought anyone. Yes, he may have already done something, but he also may not have! I want to call the police, the army, the damn U.S. Marines, but as long as that unknown is there, I just can't take that chance." She reached across the table and grabbed hold of her girl's hands. "Now I'm asking you as your best friend, for the last time . . . please just watch over my girls until I get back or call. Please? Before I leave I need to know that you will do that for me."

Jess looked at her friend with desperate eyes. Melissa was right; she needed to call for help. But she just couldn't because if the slightest chance of saving Esias's life existed, then she had no choice but to play by Jayson's rules. It was a frighteningly difficult decision to stick to, but it was one she couldn't stray from, and as she held onto Melissa's hands and looked at her, she prayed that her friend would acquiesce and make the same decision.

She stared, her eyes unblinking, imploring. Melissa stared back, the decision difficult for Jess to see in hers.

"Please?" Jess asked again.

Melissa watched her, and after a few more seconds, shook her head, let out a long breath of air, and said, "If you were anybody else, there's no way I would be giving in."

Jess smiled as a small bit of tension fell away from her shoulders, which were still very much taut with worry. "Thank you."

Melissa took a deep breath and exhaled. "You have until dawn, Jess. That's all I can give you. If I don't hear from or see you and Esias together by dawn, then I will be calling the goddamned cavalry. OK?"

Jess gave Melissa a nod. "OK."

"You better be back, girl . . . both of you."

Jess looked at her. Tears had welled in her friend's eyes. "I will," she said, a knot rising in her throat.

"You better."

Jess gave Melissa's hand a firm but gentle squeeze, then let go and stood up.

"Dawn," Melissa said, wiping tears away from the bottom of her eyes.

Jess gave a tiny smile, turned, and left the kitchen. She went upstairs to her daughters' bedroom. She had to see them, needed to see them before she left. She needed to give them kisses. Needed to smell them, to touch them.

She walked into their room quietly and approached their twin beds, which lay side by side. She watched them sleep for a moment, watched them breathe. *Angels*, she thought as tears began to fall from her eyes. Angels who didn't deserve to have their lives devastated by her stupidity. She wiped her tears away and leaned down toward them. "I love you," she whispered, planting gentle kisses on each one of their foreheads. "I promise I'm going to bring Daddy home."

She gently stroked their hair, and then left the room and went back downstairs, where Melissa was waiting for her by the front door. She put the Steelers' cap back on and went to her friend. "Thank you," she said again.

Melissa gave her a thin-lipped smile. "What are you going to do when you get there?" she asked.

Jess looked at her friend and answered as honestly as she could with a shrug. "I don't know. But I'll do whatever I have to."

Melissa looked at her, confliction in her eyes. "I really shouldn't give in to you," she said with the corner of her lips turned downward. "But since I am . . ." She paused momentarily and raised her hand. In it she wielded a small handgun. "The least I can do is make sure you're prepared to do just that."

Jess looked down at the gun and felt her blood grow cold.

"Take this with you. It's reliable, accurate, and, despite its size, it carries plenty of power. It's one of the best small guns on the market."

Jess stared at the small black gun for a few seconds, and then looked up at her friend. "You . . . you own a gun?"

"I have three, actually," Melissa said.

Jess slammed her brows together and gave her head a slight shake. "Three? When did you . . ." she paused. She'd never known this about her friend.

"Do you remember my ex, Nikolas?"

Jess gave a nod. Melissa met Nikolas at a social gathering for professional single Greeks one evening. They'd hit things off fairly quickly and after six months, Melissa had actually used the word *marriage* a few times in her sentences. But then as quickly as things happened for them, they fell apart just as fast six months after that when Melissa discovered that she wasn't the only female that Nikolas had used that word with.

"He was into guns and used to take me out to the range with him. It was scary at first, and then became completely exhilarating. I've been an aficionado since."

"Wow," Jess said. "I never knew."

"It's not something I really advertise."

"Wow." Jess looked down at the gun again, and then looked back. "I've never used a gun before."

"And hopefully you won't have to tonight. Especially since the repercussions for carrying an unlicensed gun in New York are so severe."

Jess thought of the football player Plaxico Burress who'd shot himself in the leg with his unlicensed gun. In for two years—the state of New York didn't play. "So then why give it to me?"

"Because . . . I'd rather fight to the death explaining to a judge and jury why you had to use a gun that wasn't yours to stay alive, as opposed to explaining to your daughters why they'll never see their mommy again."

Jess looked from her friend to the gun again. A chill came over her. A gun. Something she'd never held before. Something she never imagined she would ever have to hold. Her eyes on the muzzle, she said, "I . . . I've never fired a gun before."

"It's not hard. Just keep your feet planted firmly, put your right foot forward if you can and your left back slightly, like this."

Jess watched mesmerized as Melissa got into a shooter's stance.

"Keep your legs spread shoulder width and keep your arms straight and locked up in a straight line into your line of vision. Most important, don't lean away from the gun if you have to fire it. Most amateurs lean away, which is pretty much the same as leaning away from the target, which, of course, means they miss. Now, this switch means the safety is on. Click it this way and the safety is off."

"Wow," Jess said again, as Melissa relaxed from her shooter's stance. "Who are you?"

Without a smile, Melissa handed Jess the gun and said, "I'm a best friend who is trying to stay true to her word."

Jess looked down at the cold hard steel in her hand for a moment, and passed her finger over the safety before she slid it into the front pocket of her hooded sweatshirt. She looked up at her friend and gave her an appreciative, tight-lipped half smile. "Dawn, right?" she said, her tone even.

Melissa looked at her long and hard, then nodded and said with a sigh, "Dawn."

Jess gave her another half smile, and then without a good-bye, grabbed her keys from a key ring beside the door and walked out of her home. What Jayson had in store for her she had no clue, but everything that was happening was her fault. To make things right, she would do whatever she had to. There was just no way around that.

Jess walked to her car, the weight of the gun tapping her belly softly as she did. She looked up as she hit the remote to unlock the car doors. The moon was out, full and intense in the dark sky. *Dawn,* she thought. *Just a few hours away.* She got in her car and drove, knowing her destination, yet not knowing it at the same time.

Chapter 47

Jayson stood still on the balcony outside of the bed-room where he and Jess had made sweet, perfect music together. It had been incredible the way he had fit inside of her. A hand in a very wet glove. Of all the women he had fucked, never before had he felt such an intense connection. The sex between them had been the culmination, the final confirmation he had needed to prove to him that there was no denying the obvious; Jess was meant to be his.

He stood still and listened to the activity of the New York streets below. He always loved New York. It had a soul that appealed to him the way no other city did.

New York.

Jess was from New York. Born and raised. More proof that they had been meant to be. His search for the one to carry on his legacy was over, and it had ended in the city that never slept.

Jayson stood. Listened. Breathed in the warm air that would never be clean. Soon, Jess would be there, and then forever could begin.

His cell phone chimed from the room behind him. Jayson turned. A text had come through. He went to his phone and saw a message from Jess that read, I'm on my way.

He replied back. The door will b unlocked. Come 2 the balcony.

He hit send, and then went back out onto the balcony and stared out at the activity of the night.

Chapter 48

Jess couldn't breathe. Despite the fact that she was taking in air in short, rapid breaths, she still could not breathe. She'd driven, she'd dealt with the stop-and-go traffic, she'd parked, she'd sat in her car for what felt like days, then she'd gotten out, walked into the hotel, took the elevator to Jayson's floor, stepped out, and walked to his door, where she now stood unmoving, all without consciously seeing, hearing, or doing any of those things.

She'd driven, yet she hadn't seen the stoplights, the traffic around her, the cars in the parking garage, the interior of the lobby, or the four walls of the elevator. She wasn't deaf, yet she hadn't heard the blaring car horns, the jazz intended to calm her down playing from her car stereo, the soft music playing in the lobby of the hotel, the ding of the elevator when it arrived on the ground floor, or when it reached Jayson's. Neither had she felt the potholes or dips of the city streets she drove on but didn't see, nor had she heard the clicking of her heels on the concrete she didn't feel as she walked through the parking garage, and then through the lobby of the hotel.

Jess saw, heard, and felt nothing except Esias's eyes, the sound of his deep voice, and the immensely heavy beating of her heart beneath her chest. Other than that, nothing registered.

Jess breathed, yet didn't, and stared at the door, which was slightly ajar thanks to a towel in the doorjamb. Her body shook as her heart raced and threatened to explode. Sweat trickled down the small of her back.

Call the police. There's still time. Call the police and let them bring the cavalry.

Jess slid her hand into the front pocket of her sweatshirt. Both her cell phone and the gun Melissa had given her were there.

Take the cell phone out and do what you need to do.

Air passed through her nostrils, went down into her lungs, and then eased back out through her nasal passages. Her heart beat like thunder as her fingers closed, not around the cell, but Melissa's gun instead. As they did, a jolt of fear, doubt, courage, and apprehension seared through her all at the same time. A gun. She couldn't believe she had it. She didn't want to have it. But she had to have it. And if it came down to it, then she would have to use it too.

She stared at the door, ajar for her to walk inside and go to the balcony, where she had let Jayson enter her from behind as she leaned forward against the stone. They'd been out admiring the sounds of New York when Jayson began to caress her breasts while he kissed the back of her neck. Her neck, her erogenous zone. He had taken her deep on that balcony. Made her moans, ooh's, and ah's blend in with the sounds of the city. It had been bold, exciting, and uninhibited.

Jess shivered and forced the recollection of that regretful moment away from her mind. Tonight, no matter what, she was determined to create a new memory. She just hoped that she would be around to recall it afterward. She pushed the door open and walked inside.

Chapter 49

Jayson heard the door to the suite creak open, and then click shut. He smiled as the hairs on his arms rose. His manhood throbbed. Jess.

Showered, shaved, and fully clothed in a black suit by Liz Claiborne, with a white button-down shirt beneath, the two top buttons undone, he sat at a small table elegantly set for two with candles in the middle, wineglasses at opposite sides, and a bottle of champagne chilling in a bucket of ice. Behind him, playing from his iPod, which sat in the base of a small portable Bose unit, was music by the group Pink Martini. He'd read a book on a whim once about a woman that had been paid by wives to ruin their marriages, and in the book, Pink Martini had been mentioned. Jayson looked them up on iTunes, and then, after enjoying what he had heard, purchased all of their songs. Their music was calm, sexy, and entrancing without even trying, just the way Jess was.

Jess.

His father had told him once that people didn't always know what was good for them. That sometimes they had to be made to realize what that was. He didn't want to hurt her, but if Jess insisted on continuing to deny the obvious the way she had over the phone, he was going to help her understand. In this life or the next.

Jayson listened to the music and waited for her to appear.

Chapter 50

Esias. He was nowhere to be found. Not within the confines of the suite, but perhaps on the balcony where soft music was coming from.

Jess took quick breaths as she moved from the small sitting area to a pair of double doors opened wide. *Please be out there*, she thought. She slid both of her hands into the pocket of her sweatshirt and wrapped the fingers of her right hand around the gun's handle.

Still time, her conscience said. *Still time to call. Don't go out there. Back away.*

Jess tightened her grip. Her palms were damp with trepidation.

Back away.

She took another breath. Quick, short as her heart galloped.

Still time.

Jess took a step. Not back, but forward. Two more and she was at the threshold.

Her conscience begged her again to *back away*. She thought about it for a fleeting second. Then, after admitting to herself she had already passed the point of no return the minute she walked out of her home with Melissa's gun, she took a deep breath, released it, and stepped forward onto the balcony.

"Hi, beautiful."

Jess turned her head to the right to see Jayson sitting at a small table set for two with candles and champagne. "Would you like a glass of champagne?"

Jess looked at him as he sat casually as though he had never threatened to do harm to the man she loved. "Where's my husband?" she asked.

Jayson stared at her for a moment, and then frowned. "Come and sit down, Jess. Please."

Jess stood firm, her eyes on him as he flashed a smile that just weeks ago she'd found sexy and smoldering. *Crazy,* she thought. As many times as they had spoken and as many times as she had looked at his pictures, she'd never seen the craziness in his eyes that she saw now. No. Not crazy. That was too subtle a word.

Insane. That was the word that applied.

She shook her head. "Where's my husband?" she asked again.

Jayson watched her, his hands resting on the table. He watched but didn't reply.

Jess demanded again, "Where's Esias?"

Jayson looked at her long and hard with a glare that made her shiver. "We talked about this over the phone," he said after a few tense seconds.

Jess felt herself grow hot and cold at the same time. "Tell me, Jayson. Tell me now where my husband is."

"Or *what?*" Jayson said, the tone of his voice becoming sharper.

She swallowed. "I'll call the police," she replied.

Jayson cracked his thumbs. "Do you *really* think I would let you do that?" He pushed his chair back and stood up. "Do you really, Jess?"

Jess watched him as he stood still, his eyes on her, his stare intense. Her heart beat fast and heavy like the patter of feet coming down hardwood stairs. Hard, fast, unforgiving.

What are you going to do when you get there? A question Melissa had asked her.

She took a short breath and thought of the gun in her sweatshirt. The gun she didn't want in her possession. She said, "Please, just tell me where Esias is."

Jayson looked at her, his jaw set, his eyes dark. Seconds of glaring passed before he answered. "Esias is dead."

Jess's heart stopped. She'd heard the words, but somehow they couldn't have been real. She shook her head slowly. "You . . . you're lying," she said, a twinge of doubt in her voice.

"No, I'm not," Jayson replied. "I shot him and left him to bleed to death in an alleyway."

Tears welled in Jess's eyes and began to trickle down. "N . . . no," she said, her throat constricting.

"He was in the way, Jess. He was distracting and confusing you. Making you believe that you and I were not meant to be."

"No . . ." Jess said as her tears ran. "No . . . No!"

"No more waiting, Jess. No more delaying the obvious."

Jess continued to shake her head as Jayson took a step away from the table. Tears were streaming from her eyes now as her knees began to weaken. She continued to deny Jayson's claim with the movement of her head, continued to say, "No! No!"

"There's nothing and no one standing in our way now, Jess."

"No! No!"

"I'm going to make you so happy, baby. Happier than you've ever been."

Jess began to tremble. She didn't want to believe him. She couldn't. Not her husband. Jayson was lying. Trying to confuse her. She refused to believe him. Esias wasn't dead. He was alive. He had to be because she'd promised her girls that she would bring him home.

"We were destined to be, Jess," Jayson said, his voice even.

What are you going to do? Melissa's question popped in her head again, louder, more insistent than before.

What was she going to do?

Jess shook her head. No! No! No!

The word repeated itself over and over in her head as she stuck her hand into the pocket of her hoodie and wrapped her fingers around Melissa's gun.

What was she going to do?

She stared at Jayson through blurred vision as she removed her hand from her pocket with the gun in her palm and pointed it at Jayson. She stood with her feet spread slightly, her arms locked straight ahead, her left hand cradling her right as her finger rested against the trigger.

The question: What was she going to do?

The answer: Whatever she had to.

"Where is my husband?" she demanded.

Jason stood still, looked from her to the gun, then looked back up at her. There was a mild expression of surprise and amusement in his eyes. "A gun," he said with a smirk. "I'm impressed."

"Where's my husband?" Jess said again, her voice stronger.

"I already told you, Jess. He's dead."

Tasting the salt from her tears on her lips, Jess shook her head and said, "You're lying!"

"Do we have to repeat this conversation again?"

"Where is he, Jayson? Tell me now!"

"Or what, Jess? You'll shoot me?"

Jess gave a frenetic nod. "Yes!"

Jayson chuckled. "No, you won't," he said watching her intensely.

"Yes, I will! If you don't tell me where Esias is right now!"

Jayson sighed. "I've already answered your question, Jess. If that's not sufficient for you, then pull the trigger and shoot me."

Jess's hand began to tremble. "I . . . I will," she said, the strength in her voice fading as did the belief that her husband was alive.

Jayson took a step forward. "Then do it," he said. "Shoot me."

"I . . . I will," she said, her hands shaking more. What was she going to do? The question kept repeating itself as Jayson took another step toward her. What was she going to do? What was she going to do?

"Do it," Jayson challenged her. "I killed Esias."

Her heart hammered as her tears rained down. *Esias, dead?* Sharp pain pulsed at her temples. *Esias, dead? No!*

"I'm going to kill you!" she screamed.

"Then do it!" Jayson screamed back as he took another step closer to her. "Shoot me!"

"I . . . I will!"

"Stop saying it and pull the fucking trigger!"

Jess let out a cry and before she realized she was doing it, she leaned forward as Melissa had instructed and squeezed the trigger.

But nothing happened.

No pop, no crack. Nothing shattered in front of, beside, or behind Jayson as he continued to walk toward her.

She squeezed the trigger again, and then whispered, "Oh no," when the realization of why nothing had happened hit her. A split second later, Jayson knocked the gun from her hand, backhanded her viciously across the mouth, and sent her reeling to the ground.

Standing above her, he said, "Rule number one when firing a weapon, Jess . . . it can't be done unless you take the safety off." He kicked her in her midsection, sending her rolling to the left. "I thought you were different, Jess," he said, kicking her again. "I thought you were special, a cut above all of the others."

Another kick.

"I can't believe I was so fucking wrong! I can't believe I ever thought you were anything more than a fucking, cheating whore!" Jayson delivered another hard blow to her ribs.

Jess gasped for breath as pain like she'd never felt before riddled through her. She was sure something had been broken.

Jayson kicked her again, and then wrapped his fingers around her throat and hoisted her from the ground. His face inches from hers, he said, "I can't believe I ever thought you were supposed to help me carry on my legacy."

As though she were nothing but a ragdoll, he tossed her to the side, sending her crashing back against the waist-high ledge of the balcony, and then rushed her and wrapped his hands around her throat again. "You played me, Jess. And I'm going to kill you for that. For making me think my search was over."

Jess grabbed his hands and tried to pry his fingers from around her throat. She was becoming dizzy and light-headed with each passing second, and she knew that if she didn't find a way to break his grasp, he was going to succeed. Spots began to appear before her eyes as she tried in vain to loosen his grasp. She let go of his fingers and hit him several times, each blow weaker than the one before it. She tried to speak, to beg for her life, but with her windpipe constricted, she could produce little more than a gurgling sound. She tried to hit him again.

Jayson laughed off each weak, futile blow, pulled her toward him, and then pushed her back hard against the ledge over and over.

Pain rifled through her back. Her head felt as though it were going to explode from the lack of oxygen. Her eyes felt as if they were going to pop out of her head, and they began to close slowly as the cold approach of death neared.

"You could have avoided this!" Jayson said. "All you had to do was choose me. Now you'll be dead along with Esias, and your girls will be left with no one!"

Jess's eyes snapped open wide. Her girls. They were home, in bed, oblivious to what was going on, oblivious to the pain and heartache that would be coming for them. To lose one parent was horrible, but to lose two . . .

Her vision foggy, she stared up at Jayson, who smiled cruelly down at her.

Her gaze fell away down to the ground, and when it did, it fell upon Melissa's gun.

Death and darkness were approaching, racing toward her, but so was a light behind it.

Jess stared at the gun.

Her heartbeat began to increase.

She had seconds to try with everything she had left.

Seconds to fight to survive, to keep her girls from experiencing the worst pain they would ever feel.

Seconds to deliver the one blow she hadn't thought of until now.

Jayson squeezed harder and smiled heartlessly, certain that her death was imminent.

Jess stared down at the gun. She begged for the strength she would need. Then she looked up at Jayson and with everything she could muster, drove her knee hard into his balls.

A momentary recognition of pain flashed in Jayson's eyes as he stared back at her before he groaned, loosened his grasp, staggered back a step, and doubled over with his hand grabbing his crotch.

Jess didn't hesitate.

Before Jayson uttered a painful "Bitch!" at her, and before she could think to take a full and much-needed breath, she dove for the gun.

Jayson cursed her again and spun around. When he did, Jess had the gun in her hand.

Jess didn't think.

She didn't aim.

She just clicked off the safety and squeezed.

This time something happened.

Chapter 51

Jayson saw the bullet coming before it hit him. The world had slowed so much that a snail's pace would have been like Usain Bolt running the one-hundred yard dash. So he saw the bullet exploding from the muzzle of the gun Jess held, saw it whizzing through the humid air, splitting specks of dirt. Saw it coming fast—with promised intent—straight for his forehead.

He thought of all the women he'd chatted with, the women he'd gotten to play his game as he searched for the right one he thought he'd found in Jess. For years he'd tried to apply his father's lessons. He'd tried to become the man that his father had been. But, as he watched the bullet come toward him, he realized he'd failed miserably because he'd chosen the wrong one.

Jess. The one that never was.

Jayson watched the bullet come. He smiled before it hit.

And then he felt nothing.

Chapter 52

Jess let the gun fall from her hands as she watched Jayson fall over onto his side. Blood ran, pooled beneath his head as his eyes stared blankly at nothing. Melissa's question ran through her mind one final time. She looked at Jayson's dead body, content with her answer.

Finally, she took a labored breath. With the adrenaline wearing off, the pain from the beating she'd taken and from the fingers choking her returned. She moaned, took another breath, and moaned again.

And then her cell phone rang from inside of her hoodie. Despite the violent kicks to her midsection, her cell phone had survived.

She reached into her front pocket, pulled out her cell, and looked at the ID. It was Melissa calling. She thought about her daughters, hit the talk button quickly, and put the phone to her ear. "M . . . Mel . . . Meli . . . ssa," she said, each syllable uttered with excruciating pain.

"Jess! Where are you?"

Jess looked up. She hadn't noticed before, but the sun was rising. Dawn had come. Tears began to fall from her eyes again. Dawn. She'd promised to be back by then with Esias. She said, "It . . . It's over. Jay . . . Jayson's . . . he's dead." She paused, not wanting to continue with more she needed to say. That despite everything, she had still failed. She'd lost her husband. "Melissa . . . I . . . I lost Esias."

She squeezed her eyes tightly as tears continued to run and put her hand to her face.

"Jess! Esias is alive!"

Jess removed her hand. "Wh . . . what?"

"Esias is alive, Jess. A boy found him in an alleyway and called 911. He's in the hospital."

"He . . . he's alive?" Jess said, stunned.

"Yes!"

Tears of joy and relief poured from Jess's eyes. Esias was alive. "How . . . how are my girls?"

"They're fine. They're with me at the hospital. Jess, are you still at the hotel?"

Jess nodded. "Yes."

"I'm calling the police."

At that moment, there was a banging at the door to the suite, and then voices yelled, indicating they were the police. Jess smiled. "N . . . no need," she said. A few seconds later, the door was kicked in. "They're here already."

Jess hit the end button and let the phone fall from her hands as the cavalry surrounded her.

Epilogue

Jess squeezed Esias's hand. They were sitting in the fifth row at the Grammy Awards. Mary J. Blige was among the nominees for song of the year, and the crowd was anxiously waiting for the winner to be announced. Mary's song was an upbeat track filled with rhythmic bass and a horn arrangement that many called genius. It was one of several of Esias's tracks on her album.

She turned and looked at her husband, a scar along his forehead catching her eye. Fortunately for him, Shane Mitchell had been hiding out in the alley when Esias had been shot and had called the police once Jayson pulled away. Had he not been there, Esias would have never survived the wound to his chest.

It had taken months of counseling, but the two of them had managed to find their way back to solid ground once more once the dust settled after Jess revealed all of the things she had done with Jayson—real name wasn't Jayson at all but rather Eric.

Jess learned from the police that his full name was Eric Barber and that he was from Detroit, Michigan. He had lived with his father, a business executive, who'd started a very successful Internet-based company during the dot-com era of the mid-nineties. His mother had died long ago, and his father had died of a heart attack when Eric was twenty-three. Before he passed, he'd decreed in his will that his only child would get everything when the day of his death came. Never interested in running a business, Eric sold the company promptly, took the millions he'd made, and lived a life filled with partying and drinking. Trouble had become the norm for Eric. So too had run-ins with the law, so much so that a life behind bars was where Eric was headed.

But then one day, he disappeared. Jayson surfaced four years later.

A persona created for reasons that investigators, family, former friends, and associates could never answer. He just existed. And along with his existence, so too did a horde of files on his laptop and PC at his home filled with nude pictures and explicit conversations from women he'd met online. Some of the women were single, but most were married women he had targeted. Through the use of a truth or dare game, he got them to say and do things they desired but could and would never admit to those closest to them. Truths were answered. Dares were completed, oftentimes in much more forceful ways than the women had requested. Many of the women wanted to go to the police when Jayson was finished with them, but when they threatened to do so, he threatened to expose their secret and "dirty" life to everyone they knew. Years passed, and no one said a word.

And then he met Jess.

Because of everything Jayson had done throughout the years, and because of what she was fighting for, Jess avoided jail time for murder and served just six months of community service in a shelter working with abused women. Melissa served the same sentence for providing Jess with the gun. As far as Jess was concerned, it was an even trade.

Jess squeezed Esias's hand again. He turned and looked at her, love radiated from his eyes. Jess leaned over and kissed her husband on his lips. The road hadn't been easy, but ultimately, everything they'd been through had made their love stronger. But given the chance to do it all over again, Jess would not.

She put her head on Esias's shoulder and closed her eyes as they announced the Grammy winner.

Book Club Discussion Guide

1. Why do you think women indulged in Jayson's game? What made Jess susceptible to it? Would you have been?

2. Why do you think Jayson played? What was the driving force for him?

3. Had it not been Jayson, do you think someone else would have grabbed Jess's attention?

4. Would you have gone to the police or would you have remained silent for fear of Jayson exposing your secrets? Were the women weak for not doing so?

5. Why do you think Candy didn't call someone for help to save Reggie's life?

6. What was the most shocking moment in the book?

7. How do you think Jayson's father influenced him?

8. Were you surprised that Jess's marriage to Esias survived? Could you have remained with your partner had you been Esias?

9. Was Melissa right or wrong for supplying the gun? Would you have taken it or would you have called the police?

10. Did Jayson get what he deserved? Did Jess?

ORDER FORM
URBAN BOOKS, LLC
78 E. Industry Ct
Deer Park, NY 11729

Name: (please print):_____

Address: _____

City/State: _____

Zip: _____

QTY	TITLES	PRICE
	16 On The Block	$14.95
	A Girl From Flint	$14.95
	A Pimp's Life	$14.95
	Baltimore Chronicles	$14.95
	Baltimore Chronicles 2	$14.95
	Betrayal	$14.95
	Black Diamond	$14.95
	Black Diamond 2	$14.95
	Black Friday	$14.95
	Both Sides Of The Fence	$14.95
	Both Sides Of The Fence 2	$14.95
	California Connection	$14.95

Shipping and handling-add $3.50 for 1st book, then $1.75 for each additional book.

Please send a check payable to:

Urban Books, LLC

Please allow 4-6 weeks for delivery

ORDER FORM
URBAN BOOKS, LLC
78 E. Industry Ct
Deer Park, NY 11729

Name: (please print):_____

Address: _____

City/State: _____

Zip: _____

QTY	TITLES	PRICE
	California Connection 2	$14.95
	Cheesecake And Teardrops	$14.95
	Congratulations	$14.95
	Crazy In Love	$14.95
	Cyber Case	$14.95
	Denim Diaries	$14.95
	Diary Of A Mad First Lady	$14.95
	Diary Of A Stalker	$14.95
	Diary Of A Street Diva	$14.95
	Diary Of A Young Girl	$14.95
	Dirty Money	$14.95
	Dirty To The Grave	$14.95

Shipping and handling-add $3.50 for 1st book, then $1.75 for each additional book.

Please send a check payable to:

Urban Books, LLC

Please allow 4-6 weeks for delivery